"Is it true?"

Hunter's voice was deep and tight and sounded like it came out through clenched teeth even as it boomed from a speaker off to her left.

With an appalled snarl, he ripped the wire from his lapel and pulled something from his pocket, handing it to the man beside him.

"Is it?" he demanded of her without the bullhorn effect.

"Of course not," she lied blatantly. "This is all a horrible misunderstanding. I'm very sorry for the interruption," she added to the crowd. Her face was boiling so ferociously in embarrassment it felt like it was about to combust. She was so dizzy she could hardly see straight.

"You just said you didn't tell me. That I didn't know," Hunter pointed out with subdued outrage.

Hunter lifted his gaze over Amelia's head.

Amelia looked over her shoulder and up.

The bride had come to the rail of the terrace. She was red-carpet gorgeous with midnight-black hair and luminous golden shoulders accentuated by the stark whiteness of her strapless satin gown. Her veil caught the sunlight so it created an angel's halo effect around her astonished yet beautiful face.

Could this moment get any worse?

Four Weddings and a Baby

You are cordially invited to...the scandal of the wedding season!

In a shocking turn of events, the marriage of billionaire Hunter Waverly, aka the groom, was halted today when it was revealed he has a secret baby with a local waitress! Their one night clearly wasn't enough...but will this be a real-life Cinderella story?

And the drama doesn't stop there. Our sources say humiliated bride Eden decided to take matters—or should we say, the diamond ring—into her own hands and eloped with best man, Remy Sylvain! Well, those two have always had a special connection since that night in Paris...

Meanwhile, maid of honor Quinn is rumored to have been whisked away by Eden's brother Micah. And the groom's sister Vienna? Let's just say, she has the biggest secret of all...

It's never a dull moment at a billion-dollar society wedding!

Read Hunter and Amelia's story in
Cinderella's Secret Baby
Available now!

Don't miss Remy and Eden's story in
Wedding Night with the Wrong Billionaire

And look out for
Micah and Quinn's story
and
Vienna and Jasper's story
Coming soon!

Dani Collins

CINDERELLA'S SECRET BABY

Recycling programs for this product may not exist in your area.

ISBN-13: 978-1-335-73871-4

Cinderella's Secret Baby

Copyright © 2022 by Dani Collins

For questions and comments about the quality of this book, please contact us at CustomerService@Harlequin.com.

Harlequin Enterprises ULC
22 Adelaide St. West, 41st Floor
Toronto, Ontario M5H 4E3, Canada
www.Harlequin.com

Printed in U.S.A.

Canadian **Dani Collins** knew in high school that she wanted to write romance for a living. Twenty-five years later, after marrying her high school sweetheart, having two kids with him, working at several generic office jobs and submitting countless manuscripts, she got The Call. Her first Harlequin novel won the Reviewers' Choice Award for Best First in Series from *RT Book Reviews*. She now works in her own office, writing romance.

Books by Dani Collins

Harlequin Presents

Her Impossible Baby Bombshell
One Snowbound New Year's Night
Innocent in Her Enemy's Bed

Jet-Set Billionaires

Cinderella for the Miami Playboy

Signed, Sealed...Seduced

Ways to Ruin a Royal Reputation

The Secret Sisters

Married for One Reason Only
Manhattan's Most Scandalous Reunion

Visit the Author Profile page
at Harlequin.com for more titles.

To my sisters, Donna and Maggie, who live far away, but are always here for me. I love you both very much.

CHAPTER ONE

AMELIA LINDOR COULDN'T fathom what had gotten into her father, Tobias. He had come straight back after leaving on his morning constitutional with a fire in his belly, insisting Amelia drive him from Goderich to Niagara-on-the-Lake. *Right now.*

It was a three-hour trip that her daughter, Peyton, had *not* enjoyed. The two-month-old believed any car ride longer than twenty minutes was intolerable torture and made sure everyone knew it. After fussing on and off for two hours, she had finally settled into a hard nap.

The silence was a blessed relief, but it threw off the schedule Amelia had finally started to establish with her. Peyton was meant to be nursing by now. As Amelia parked and bent into the back seat of her dusty but trusty sedan, her breasts were already heavy and tight. Should she wake the baby and coax her to feed? Or risk a public letdown?

"How long will we be here?" Amelia asked her father, but only got a slammed door in response. She stood and called, "Dad?"

"I told you, I have to meet someone," he grumbled over his shoulder as he hurried through the full parking lot toward the door of the winery's tasting house.

"Who?" she said with exasperation.

He didn't answer. Or wait. Tobias had arthritis and a heart weakened by grief, but seconds later he had heaved open the wide door and disappeared inside.

This didn't make sense. When her father met someone, it was usually his fellow retirees from the salt mine. Six mornings a week, he rose to take his medication, record the temperature in his weather journal and listen to the early news. He left as soon as it was light, joining his buddies at the café two streets over where they nursed coffee and grudges against politicians and potholes.

This morning, one of his cronies had said something that sent him home to snap orders like the maintenance supervisor Tobias had once been. *Let's go. This can't wait.*

Since Amelia's only plan for the day had been drop-in infant yoga, she had hurriedly dressed, and here they were.

Tobias had refused to talk in the car, so she had bounced through the music stations, trying to calm Peyton, remaining ignorant as to what this was all about.

Releasing an irked sigh, she carefully skimmed the limp Peyton into her arms. Since the seat weighed more than her baby did, she only threw a receiving blanket over her shoulder and cradled Peyton there, not even bothering with the diaper bag so she could hurry after her father.

A couple came out the door as Amelia approached, both dressed to the nines. The man wore a dapper suit; the woman was in a strapless amethyst gown. Bridesmaid. Who else dressed like that at eleven twenty in the morning? Was that why there had been purple and pearl balloons on the welcome sign?

The woman abruptly halted before crashing into Amelia. She offered a strained smile that suggested a supreme effort at politeness when she was barely holding on to her temper.

"Hello. Vienna. Sister of the groom." She touched her bare upper chest, then gestured into the tasting room. "Go all the way through and out the back. You'll see the pergola by the shore. Everyone is sitting down. We're about to start."

"I'm not here for a wedding." Amelia grimaced an apology as she realized they were intruding on a ceremony. "My father is—" On a rampage of some sort. "Inside. Looking for someone."

"Oh?" Vienna cocked her head. "Who? We've reserved the entire place for the wedding. I might know them."

"I'm not sure, but we'll get out of your hair right away. I promise." Amelia turned her friendly smile up to the man still holding the door. Cool, conditioned air beckoned from inside. "Thank you."

"My pleasure," he said in the very creepy tone some men used when they thought they were being charming by sexually harassing a woman. His gaze slid down to ogle the stretched neckline of her T-shirt. The pink cotton was straining across her nursing bra, but one breast was squashed by her *newborn baby* so, *Don't be gross, man*, Amelia thought crossly.

Behind her, Vienna was saying an impatient, "Okay, Neal. What's so important you had to drag me out here when it's about to start?"

The door closed behind her, and Amelia blinked in the shadowed interior, turning over the name Vienna in her mind. It was unusual, but she had heard it somewhere, which caused a prickle of premonition.

At the same time, the sounds and smells of the tasting room were provoking a flashback. Last summer, Amelia had taken a job at a microbrewery not far from here. On her off days, she and her workmates had toured the local wineries on their bicycles, getting tipsy inside tasting rooms like this one with its brick floor and post-and-beam ceiling. This was a bigger vineyard, so the tasting room had two bars, one on either side. Behind each were rows and rows of bottles, while the space between was full of shelves displaying knickknacks and branded tea towels and specialty wineglasses.

Amelia automatically blocked the other memories that tried to invade from last July. The ones containing a brooding man who had kissed her in the moonlight and warned her against coming to his room.

My life is a mess right now. It won't be more than tonight.

She shifted the weight of that encounter to her

other shoulder as she searched for Tobias. He wasn't among the guests scrambling for a glass of wine before they headed out the doors to the ceremony. Had he gone to the lawn? *Was* he meeting one of the wedding guests?

"Grandma. There's one more. Would you like to sign the guest book?" An adorable girl of eight or nine reopened the book she had closed. She stood behind an upended barrel near the door and wore a demure version of the bridesmaid's dress. Her hair was gathered up in a bundle of tight black curls on her crown, and she wore a hint of soft pink makeup on her lips and cheeks. She had clearly been given this Very Special Job and was taking it *very* seriously.

An older woman wearing a stylish royal blue dress gave the girl an indulgent look before saying to Amelia, "Welcome. Friend of the bride or groom?"

"I'm not here for the wedding." That ought to be obvious from her very casual clothes. Her stomach was starting to sour at how ill-timed her father's mission was. "Did you see an older man come through? He's wearing a yellow shirt and brown pants. He has a bushy gray beard?"

"I think so." The little girl's face screwed up quizzically and she looked to her grandmother. "He didn't sign, either."

"He said he had an important message for the groom. I sent him to the guesthouse." The older woman pointed down a hall where a glass door led to a covered walkway. "The groomsmen were gathering for a sip of courage in the breakfast room." She winked. "Would you excuse us? Hannah and I need to take our seats."

"Of course. Thank you." Amelia turned to start down the hall, but her gaze was snagged by the chalkboard behind the bar.

The stark black slate was adorned with a border of silk orchids in purple and white. Calligraphed letters read Congratulations Hunter and Eden.

Amelia's heart jolted to a stop, then slammed into a panicked gallop.

No. No, Dad. No.

Nooooo.

"I've always presumed I would get married at my aunt's vineyard," Hunter Waverly's fiancée had said when their engagement became official. "Weddings are their specialty. She'll pull out all the stops for me."

Hunter had gone along because a groom didn't override his bride when she set her heart on an outdoor wedding at a vineyard on a lake. Holding the ceremony here had been one less decision. Simple, if not ideal.

By anyone's standards, everything about this wedding was perfect. Bright June sunshine beamed from a cloudless sky. There was a soft breeze coming off the water, just enough to keep Hunter from overheating in his suit as he walked out to the pergola. If any of the typical day of disasters had occurred behind the scenes, solutions had been found before Hunter heard a whisper of it.

The guests were taking their seats, the bride was said to be ready, and the officiant was motioning to the string trio to wrap up their current piece.

It was unfolding flawlessly, but Hunter was tense enough to snap in half.

PTSD, he thought dourly. For most of his life, every special occasion had turned into an embarrassing disaster. He had been tempted to insist on a small ceremony with Eden, but that would have been cowardly.

The officiant checked in with his best man. Remy nodded, patting his lapel, smile tight. Something had been eating at him for months. Hunter noticed it at the engagement party, but Remy didn't want to talk about it and Hunter had lived with so little privacy in his own life, he didn't invade others'.

Through the amplifier that would allow the guests to hear their vows, he heard Eden's voice ask, "Is it working?" Her tone was a fraction higher than normal.

Wedding jitters. A bride was entitled, and Hunter refused to catch a case of it. This marriage was advantageous for both of them.

Eden had inherited controlling interest in Bellamy Home & Garden last year. Its stock value had languished in recent years, but it was a trusted Canadian icon, especially in rural communities. Eden would right the ship once she had Waverly cash at her disposal. The fact that their marriage merger included a plan to use Bellamy as a road map to bring

Wave-Com's next generation of wireless technology into all those remote locations wouldn't hurt, either.

For his part, Hunter was repairing the Waverly reputation by attaching himself to the Bellamy name. Wave-Com had suffered in the years after his father died, plagued by ugly legal fights and a takeover attempt as his stepmother had sought to steal the corporation from her husband's children, throwing mud every chance she got.

Today would turn the page on those perpetual scandals. With this sophisticated wedding, brimming with homegrown celebrities and dynasties from abroad, Hunter was setting a tone of respectability, family values and stability. Dare he add, *class*? Because Eden was intelligent, cultured and accomplished. She was well known for her philanthropy and admired for her Canadian-made fashion choices. Her grandfather had been a beloved voice on the national radio waves, and her mother still contributed weekly gardening tips to one of their programs.

Eden was suitable in other ways, too. Vienna had introduced them, implicitly promising that family gatherings would always be pleasant and civilized. Eden wanted babies right away, and Vienna was ready to start her family, too. Their children would grow up together.

Best of all, Hunter found Eden attractive, but not *too* attractive. They would have a foundation of friendship and respect, not fickle love or treacherous lust. Hunter wouldn't be tugged around by his fly the way his father had been, subjected to spectacles every other week while making excuses for the source of his humiliation.

This marriage was exactly the right thing for all concerned.

Yet his gut was full of gravel, and he couldn't shake this sense of impending doom.

It was the location. As Hunter breathed the scent of newly mown grass and heard the ducks on the lake and the buzz of bees, more prurient memories were accosting him. A musical laugh and a soft shoulder under his lips. Fine hair that carried a fragrance of sunshine.

That one night had been an escape, he often reminded himself. In some ways, it had been a narrow escape, because the heat in his blood had nearly made him say rash, embarrassing things. *Don't go in to work. I'll stay another night.* For sex.

Stop it. What kind of groom awaited his bride with a one-night stand clouding his thoughts?

Maybe it was the natural reckoning of a wedding day. He was saying goodbye to freedom and flings as he committed the rest of his life—his sex life—to one person. That heaviness in his gut wasn't misgiving. Or regret. It wasn't.

The music faded to expectant silence. The murmuring crowd quieted.

The officiant covered her lapel microphone with her hand and asked, "Ready?"

Hunter drew the device from the pocket of his coat and turned it on, noting the green light. He nodded and brushed his jacket straight again. He looked over the guests. There were roughly two hundred arranged on either side of the carpeted aisle, all smiling with anticipation.

The first notes of their wedding playlist were plucked from the harp. He looked to the top of the stairs from the terrace where his cousin's tot of three years appeared in a flouncy dress. A bridesmaid of fourteen, one of Eden's cousins, kept a firm hold of the little one's hand and used the other to hold the rail as they began to descend.

"You!"

The gravelly bellow cut through the sublime moment, creating a stillness that silenced the angelic notes and the rustling leaves on the nearby rows of vines. Even the lap of water on the shore seemed to hold its breath.

Then a higher, feminine, anguished voice broke in.

"Daddy, no. *Please.*"

CHAPTER TWO

IT WAS THE sort of wedding Amelia's blue-collar roots could only dream of.

As she glanced from the walkway, she saw pots of gardenias and begonias stationed at the ends of rows of white chairs. The posts and slatted roof of a pergola were draped in wisteria. The backdrop was a stunning view of the lake and a hazy glimpse of Toronto's skyline, like a tiny floating island, sat on the horizon.

To the right of the pergola, there was an arched walking bridge over a trickling creek, perfect for photos of the bride and groom before they made their way to the pavilion filled with rustic tables set with linen and china and sparkling crystal.

It was fairy-tale-perfect, and her father was *ruining* it.

Amelia swerved off the walkway to intercept Tobias as he came out of the guesthouse and charged toward the pergola. Everyone swiveled their attention to her, making her feel extra clumsy as she kept a firm hold on Peyton while trying not to trip on the grass.

Oh, God, look at him. Hunter Waverly was so blindingly handsome in his morning suit, clean-shaven and tall with his wide shoulders and his stern, narrow face, he made her eyes sting. From the concrete pad of the pergola, he was even taller and looked down his bladelike nose at Tobias before shifting his gaze to Amelia as she rushed up behind her father.

Hunter stood in dappled shade, but she thought he jolted as he recognized her.

She felt naked then. And small. Smaller even than when she'd left his guest room last year. Her face was blistered by that old humiliation and this new one. Her heart was cracking down the center, falling open to pulse unprotected because her *baby* was exposed. Here. In front of hundreds of eyes where their very different positions in life were even more pronounced than they had been then.

Hunter had bought out a vineyard for his bride. He had only offered *her* what was in his wallet.

"You," her father said again, voice dripping with contempt. He avoided Amelia's attempt to catch his arm. "You ignore your own flesh and blood, leave the mother of your child to fend for herself while you…" His impatient hand waved with disdain at the guests, the tranquil setting and the loving union that was about to be blessed.

"Daddy, *please.* I am *begging* you." Amelia managed to catch a fistful of his sleeve and tugged. "Come on. We're leaving. I am so sorry."

The kindly grandmother was staring at Amelia as though she was a skunk that had waddled into the kitchen. Amelia couldn't make herself look at anyone else, especially Hunter. Her stomach had risen to churn in the back of her throat.

"She's better off without you." Her father shook off her grip. "But your friends and family ought to know what sort of man you are. Your *wife* should know what she's marrying. And I'll be damned if you won't even feed and clothe the child you made." Her father shook his finger at Hunter. "Judging by this, you can afford to, so quit being a bum."

"Dad!" she cried. "He didn't know. Okay? I never told him." And if she didn't have the helpless bundle of Peyton snuggled in her arm, she would wish herself dead right now. She really would.

Someone in the crowd guffawed a curse of enjoyment.

Her father snapped a look at her. "A man has a right to know, Amelia."

"*I* have a right to decide what happens to *my* baby." She was furious with him.

"I care what happens to *my* baby," he barked straight back.

He did. She knew that. He was a dear, loving father, but *such* a dinosaur sometimes. Old-school and old-fashioned and so protective after losing Jasper, but how did he even know Hunter's name? How had he known Hunter would be here?

"Is it true?" Hunter's voice was deep and tight and sounded like it came out through clenched teeth even as it boomed from a speaker off to her left.

Oh *God*.

With an appalled snarl, he ripped the wire from his lapel and pulled something from his pocket, handing it to the man beside him.

"Is it?" he demanded of her without the bullhorn effect.

"Of course not," she lied blatantly. "This is all a horrible misunderstanding. I'm very sorry for the interruption," she added to the crowd. Her face was about to combust, it was boiling so ferociously in embarrassment. Her head was dizzy. She could hardly see straight.

"You just said you didn't tell me. That I didn't know," Hunter pointed out with subdued outrage.

Take the free pass, you idiot.

"Hunter." The man beside him—Remy, Amelia recalled—nudged Hunter.

Hunter lifted his gaze over Amelia's head.

Amelia looked over her shoulder and up.

The bride had come to the rail of the terrace. She was red-carpet-gorgeous with midnight-black hair and luminous golden shoulders accentuated by the stark whiteness of her strapless satin gown. Her veil caught the sunlight so it created an angel's halo effect around her astonished yet beautiful face.

Could this moment get any worse?

Hell, yes, Peyton assured her. She began to stir

and whimper, rubbing her face into Amelia's neck, rooting for the nipple she wanted.

Amelia's full breasts were ready. So ready.

No. Please no.

But the tightness in her heavy breasts became a hard sting. A rush of tears rose to her eyes as letdown happened. Damp warmth began soaking into the pads of her bra, leaking around the edges to stain her shirt.

Mortified, Amelia spun and started back to the walkway.

Behind her, she heard something drop like a shoe.

She glanced back to see that the bride's bouquet, a spray of ivory rosebuds interspersed with baby's breath and lacy fronds of spring ferns, had landed on the grass.

Hunter wished he were a stranger to outrageous public displays.

Sadly, this pageantry was all too familiar. His sister was equally familiar. With a sharp nod from the terrace, Vienna assured him she would stay with Eden and followed his bride back into the honeymoon suite.

Through the speakers, Eden's voice cried, "Is it *true*?"

With a squeeze of his arm, Remy also conveyed, *I've got this.* He cut a sharp line across his throat, indicating to the wedding planner that the microphone feeds should be cut.

Hunter left the pergola and brushed past the older

man still working his mouth in search of further words to berate him.

As he went after the woman who may or may not be holding his baby, Hunter's mind raced. No fully formed thoughts seemed to stick. That wasn't like him. He knew how to grasp hold of catastrophe and mitigate it. He'd been doing it since his eleventh birthday party, the first occasion his stepmother had ruined with her obscene behavior and the last time he had celebrated that annual milestone.

Get things back on course, he kept thinking, but his "course" was marriage. To Eden. He couldn't let that be derailed by a woman he had fooled around with once. Okay, three times. It had been a very active night, but it had only been sex. Not conception. Surely not.

"The woman with the baby," he snapped at one of the servers in the tasting room even as he looked to the exit to the parking lot. "Did she leave?"

"She asked for somewhere to sit and—"

Hunter stopped listening and followed the pointed finger around the corner, stalking through a closed door labeled Operations Manager.

"Excuse me." Amelia glared from the love seat crammed beneath the window.

Her face was bright red. The dark roots of her hair were so long, only the fraying bun on the top of her head was still blond. She looked a lot younger without the makeup she'd worn when he'd met her. Her brows were pulled into a knot of affliction, her wide mouth pinched.

"Get out," she said more insistently.

While nothing was on show, she was clearly uncomfortable as she cradled the nursing baby against one breast and held a pink blanket against the other.

Hunter swore, but he'd seen a baby nurse before, and this was more important.

"Is it true?" he demanded.

"Get out!"

He rolled his eyes and turned to face the closed door, stepping forward to lock it.

"I'll insist on a test either way, but I don't have time for games. There's a woman next door who deserves to know." *He* deserved to know.

Amelia muttered something and said, "Ouch. Yes, I know." She seemed to be talking to the baby because there was a cry of protest then, "There. All better." She sighed.

Silence resumed, broken by loud gulps.

As he warily turned back to face her, Hunter was doing some quick and dirty math, trying to work out if this was even possible. Nine months from July would take the birth to April.

Amelia had draped the blanket over her shoulder, and the baby was now hidden beneath the tent. One bare foot was kicking out from beneath it, working an invisible pump. Amelia kept her glower aimed at his shoes.

"How old is...?" He? She? Check that gender bias, he reminded himself. A child. Could he have made this baby?

"Nine weeks. Almost ten," Amelia admitted sullenly.

May. *June.*

Hunter swore again, using a clear, all-purpose curse that encompassed the act that had brought him to this point and the complexity of his reaction. It spanned everything from resignation to disgrace. Irony to self-disgust. Anger to injustice. Remorse.

And, flittering around the edges, a nascent curiosity coupled with a small resentment that she had hidden the baby for months. From his eyes right now.

"I didn't mean for this to happen," she mumbled. "Any of this."

"Why didn't you tell me before today?"

"I tried." Her voice grew tougher. Belligerent. "I called your office, trying to reach you. You texted back that you were engaged. You told me not to text again."

"That's not trying. For God's sake, Amelia. I wanted to hear *that.* Why did you wait... What? Five months after we were together?" He had been engaged by then. "Why didn't you tell me as soon as you found out you were pregnant?"

"I did."

He snorted, never quite believing those *I didn't know I was pregnant* urban legends.

Her lashes finally came up. Her lake-blue eyes were pools of sorrow.

"Do you remember I left that morning because Dad got the news my brother had disappeared? That's all I could think about. Finding him. When the company quit trying, I decided to go to Chile myself. I needed shots to travel, and the doctor had to screen me for pregnancy before he could administer them. I thought stress was making me sick and stopping my periods. I wasn't doing anything except sitting at a computer, writing emails, so the weight gain didn't seem unusual. We used condoms," she reminded, waving between them. "It didn't occur to me I could be pregnant."

He always used condoms and didn't recall one breaking. It seemed far-fetched that she could have gotten pregnant by him, but he was having trouble hanging on to his skepticism in the face of how upset she seemed.

"I wanted to have her, even though it meant I couldn't travel." She rubbed her brow, mouth pulled down at the corners with deep sadness. "It was the hardest decision I've ever made, but I knew Jasper would never expect me to give up a baby to go look for him, especially if…"

The catch of torment in her voice struck Hunter straight in the chest, rocking him back on his heels. He tried to imagine making a decision between his unborn child and looking for his sister. His mind refused to go there. The idea of it, the fact that Amelia had chosen to keep his baby rather than search for someone she loved, caused a visceral shift inside his chest, one that hurt in a way he didn't understand.

He brushed aside trying to untangle that emotive knot, focusing instead on the word "her." Such a tiny detail, but now he knew that little foot belonged to a girl. His daughter?

"I thought I should tell you, but you blew me off,"

Amelia said in a lifeless tone. "Given all I was going through, it seemed like a blessing that you didn't want to be involved. One less person to worry about."

You didn't ask *me if I wanted to be involved*, he nearly growled, but she was obviously still in deep pain, so he bit that back.

"And your brother?" he probed carefully.

"Presumed dead."

Hunter rubbed the cynicism from his expression. "I'm sorry, Amelia. That's rough."

"It is. Dad was in pieces. I moved back into his house, we pulled up the drawbridge, and we've been looking after each other ever since. Peyton's been a bright spot, though." One side of her mouth went up a little as she caught the bare foot that was still working thin air. "Dad's been more like his old self since she arrived."

Peyton. He had a daughter named Peyton. It didn't seem real.

"And maybe we don't live like you do, but we're *fine*," she insisted. "He shouldn't have made it sound like we're starving. Dad has a pension, and the house is paid for. I get maternity benefits that I supplement by tutoring. I'm finishing my Bachelor of Ed online. In a year or so, I'll be a teacher. That's a perfectly good living for a single mom."

"But you let your father believe *I* don't care if you're starving and destitute." That rankled. A lot.

"I don't even know how he found out your name! I didn't tell anyone. Not even Cheryl— You remember her? She's the one Remy—"

"I remember," Hunter dismissed, vaguely recalling a bubbly redhead.

"I haven't really talked to her since I left," Amelia continued in a distracted mumble, lashes lifting warily. "I don't post about Peyton. No one knows you're her father."

Yeah. Not even me.

"But Dad got after me to make a will the minute she was born, especially since Jasper didn't have one. I finalized it a couple weeks ago. Maybe he read the copy I left in the freezer? I only mentioned you as a last resort. My cousin agreed to raise her if something happens. She lives in Ottawa, but she and Dad would work something out."

"I'm a last resort for custody of my child? Wow." Very few things got under his skin. Hunter had been exposed to every possible slight at one time or another. He was jaded and impervious, but that was a kick in the stomach. "What about her birth certificate? Is my name on that?"

"No." Her reply was prompt and remorseless. "I would have needed your permission, so it didn't make sense to add you. Can you turn around again? She's finished and I need to put myself back together."

He turned his back and absorbed everything she'd said, but kept coming back to that phrase, "last resort." He'd been tangled up in a legal mess for the last few years, but did that make him so objectionable a person she didn't want him to have anything to do with his own child? He was gainfully employed and didn't have a criminal record. He was about to marry—

He swore and pinched the bridge of his nose.

What the hell was he supposed to do? Parts of the merger might be salvaged if he called off the wedding, if Eden could stand to speak to the man who jilted her. She didn't deserve this humiliation any more than he did.

"I need a paternity test," he muttered, grasping at the off chance this was a stunt organized by his stepmother, but he knew. Deep down, he already knew the truth.

"I'll agree to that, but I don't expect anything from you. If you want access, we can talk about it, but please don't feel obligated."

"Of course I'm obligated, Amelia. Do you know who I *am*?" He pivoted around again to see her shirt was down and she held the baby against the blanket on her shoulder.

Peyton's fine brown hair was thin on top and turned up in feathery ducktails around the fringe, like a balding old man on a hot summer's day. In response to Amelia's pats, she released a robust burp.

Amelia was glaring at him with resentment.

"Please don't accuse me of getting pregnant for money. If that's what I wanted, I would have come after you a lot sooner."

"I've already deduced that." Everything she was saying added up to preferring to keep this baby from him. Which made him furious. And uncomfortable.

"Please don't sue me to try to take her." She tucked her chin, brows low with warning.

"Is that why you didn't tell me? You think I would try to separate my baby from her *parent*? I'm not like that, Amelia," he said pointedly.

Her scowl deepened. "I'm not going to apologize. You are in love with someone else, Hunter. About to be married. I did what I thought was right."

"By whom? Not our daughter," he scoffed. "My life comes with a lot of comfort and privilege. Your father is right. My child deserves to benefit from what I can give her."

"Her needs are met," she insisted. "She's chubby and happy and sleeps in a dry diaper under a sound roof every night. I love her to death. So does my dad. She wants for nothing."

"Except the father who wants to be part of her life. Were you really going to wait until she was old enough to ask about me before you sprang her on me?"

"I refuse to feel guilty over the choices I've made! You told me not to text you."

He brushed that aside. "If she's a Waverly, she's entitled to live like one." That much he knew.

"Fine. Organize a paternity test. Make whatever arrangements you want for her. For *her*," she stressed. "I need to live with Dad and look after him." She inched to the edge of the love seat. "And, um, don't think this is me being a jerk or anything, but I plan to talk to a lawyer and find out my rights.

She's still nursing. I genuinely think it's better if she's with me full time. I'm open to something more balanced after she weans. I want to be reasonable."

"Nice to know," he said facetiously. "But nothing about this is reasonable. It's outrageous."

She sighed. "You're right that I should have told you sooner," she admitted grudgingly. "I'm sorry it happened like this. I'll get Dad and we'll leave and—"

"And what? The damage is done," he snapped.

"To the wedding? Why? This isn't your fault. You didn't know." She blinked incredibly naive blue eyes.

"I know *now*. Everyone does." The press was going to have a field day. The clock in his head was warning that he was losing his chance to get ahead of this. The feeding frenzy had likely already started. Despite his best security precautions, there had been several boats on the water. He would bet at least a few guests or staff were already texting or posting. This was a situation ripe for one of those real-time threads that went viral.

The groom's sidepiece just showed up. Her dad brought his proverbial shotgun.

Hunter slapped a hand to his lapel, double-checking he hadn't been on a hot mic this entire time.

What would be said about this relationship? Nothing flattering. Amelia wasn't the sharp-witted, confident woman he'd met last summer, the one with straightened blond hair, cat's-eye liner and long tanned legs beneath a saucy skort.

She'd become a disheveled and distressed new mother. Her complexion was wan, and she had dark circles under her eyes—standard for new parents from what he'd heard, but it made her look extra vulnerable, and that faded T-shirt and her bargain yoga pants screamed neglect on his part.

She looked hellish, really, but there was still a clench inside him that he was fighting to ignore. *Want.* The baby weight made her curvier, which he found intriguing. The huskiness of emotion in her voice kept calling up the sensation of her soft cries spilling against his ear. From the second she had appeared, some animalistic part of him had growled with satisfaction at being near her again.

No. She had just turned his life into a mile-long train wreck. This woman was dangerous. She was everything he *didn't* want.

"What?" Amelia's gaze grew apprehensive as she realized he was staring at her. She pressed back into the love seat, cradling the baby closer.

A knock at the door had him snarling, "Busy."

"It's me," Vi said.

Amelia sucked in a worried breath, perhaps expecting Eden, but he swung around to let his sister in.

"Eden needs to know what's going on." She looked at Amelia with curiosity. "The B-Team is assembled online when you're ready."

Hunter would have given up his firstborn to never hear those words again, he thought with dark irony, but he was grateful Vi had put their PR bomb squad on standby.

The clock had run out. Decisions had to be made. He squeezed Vi's arm and left.

CHAPTER THREE

AMELIA WATCHED VIENNA close the door and lock it. She came toward her, then leaned over her to drop the blinds down the window behind her.

Amelia snorted. "Are you *hiding* me?"

"I'm protecting the newest member of our family." Vienna's brows went up with indignation. "If it's true? Please be honest, because I'm about to bond with my niece or nephew."

Now that Amelia was clued in, she saw Vienna's resemblance to Hunter in her tall bearing and dark brown hair. She had his high cheekbones and darned if her cupid's bow of a mouth wasn't exactly like Peyton's. That's where she had heard her name. Remy had said it last year. *What does Vienna think?*

Peyton was fully charged after her nap and meal. She was digging her toes into Amelia's stomach and pushing her little arms against Amelia's chest, causing her downy head to bobble against the hand Amelia kept protectively cupped behind her neck.

Vienna was looking at Peyton with hungry wistfulness, so Amelia turned her and sat her in her lap.

"It's true. This is Peyton. She turns ten weeks on Tuesday."

"Oh." Vienna's tension melted as she sank to a crouch before them. "Hello, sweet pea." Vienna beamed at Peyton and touched the baby's hand, gently clasping tiny fingers when Peyton reflexively closed her fist around her finger. "You're just the most perfect thing, aren't you?" Her thumb stroked the back of Peyton's dimpled knuckles.

Amelia's heart turned over at how tender Vienna sounded. It gave her hope they might— Well, it was probably a stretch to imagine they could become friends.

"*Please* let her know I didn't mean to ruin her special day."

"Eden?" Vienna's expression cooled and became unreadable. "It's better she knows before they marry."

"Does that mean—?" Amelia's heart lurched. "She still wants to marry him?" That was good, wasn't it? Then he wouldn't blame her for ruining his future.

So why did she feel as though her own future had just dropped into the bottom of that lake out there?

Vienna carefully withdrew from Peyton's grip and gave Peyton's round cheek a last caress before she pushed to stand over them.

"I don't know what they'll decide. I do know that calling off a wedding isn't as easy as it sounds." She bit her lip pensively. "Especially when there's so much at stake."

Amelia suddenly recalled the conflict she had walked through on arrival. She had an urge to ask Vienna if she was all right, but Vienna was smiling at Peyton again, catching her foot to give it a gentle squeeze.

"Whatever happens, I'm happy to meet you, Peyton. Every cloud has a silver lining, and you are today's."

Did that make Amelia the ominous, unwanted thunderhead?

She mustered a weak smile, growing overwhelmed as she realized Peyton had more than a father now. She had an extended family and, if Hunter married Eden, there would be step-relations who were all strangers to Amelia, yet they would all imagine they had a right to tell Hunter how he ought to raise *Amelia's* daughter.

Her pulse rate picked up, and adrenaline returned to her veins.

"Do you know where my dad is?" Amelia rose, trying not to let her voice reveal her panic, but she heard how shrill she sounded. Her shock was wearing off, and she was starting to fall apart. "I should make sure he's okay. I can't believe I left him out there with everyone."

"He's having a drink with my grandfather," Vienna said, as if that was a totally normal thing after objecting to a wedding.

"Okay, well, Peyton needs the diaper bag," she lied.

"Let me hold her while you get it." Vienna started to extend her arms.

"You can't ruin your dress. What if the wedding is back on? Dad and I should really go." Really.

"But Hunter will want—"

Amelia didn't care what Hunter wanted. She needed to get the hell away from here. She walked back to the tasting room, which had filled up with excited, babbling guests.

The walk of shame had never been so literal as when she approached her father at the bar. He was talking to a man his age in a pin-striped brown suit. They faced each other, elbows propped on the polished quartz, holding glasses of red wine. Amelia heard something about lake trout as she approached.

"Dad? Sorry," she threw at the other man, aware she was being rude. "But if you're coming home with me, the car is leaving."

She ignored his admonishing, "Amelia," and headed for the exit.

Outside, she walked through a handful of people who were smoking and laughing. One said, "Oh, hey. Can I talk to you for a minute?"

She veered around the man, fighting to wait until she was in her car and driving away before she let the tears overflow. Her throat was on fire with suppressed anguish, though.

The damned car was too hot! She had forgotten to put up the reflecting screen, so the full sun had beamed through the back window onto the car seat, heating up all the plastic and metal parts. The car itself was an oven.

With a whimper, Amelia shifted to squeeze behind the wheel long enough to start the car and set the air-conditioning to high. She closed the door and left it slightly ajar so she didn't lock herself out.

The man had followed her and tried to approach her as she stood in the shade of a nearby tree. Was he really recording her with his phone? Her heart tripped and she turned her back on him, sheltering Peyton with the angle of her body.

Thankfully, her father came out, but he only wanted to lecture her on her manners.

"What was that about? Ubert was being very decent about all of this. We thought you would need time to work something out with Hunter, so why are you leaving?"

"Dad," she hissed. "Remember how you refused to talk about this until we got here? I'm not talking about it until we get home. Also, those people are listening," she added, glaring past him at that hideous man who was edging closer like a feral dog hoping for a dropped sandwich.

Tobias glanced over his shoulder and grunted his disgust.

"How did you know he was here anyway?" she was compelled to ask, but she kept her voice pitched low. She deliberately didn't stalk Hunter online, only occasionally reading headlines in the news related to Wave-Com.

"I gave Mo the details from your will. He used that tablet his son gave him, told me Hunter was here last year when you were working here. Then he saw the notice he was getting hitched today. It seemed my best chance to catch him in person and give him a piece of my mind. How have you not told him about Peyton? It's not like you to lie to me. Is it?" His good eye fixed on her.

"It's complicated." And humiliating enough to turn her voice vehement. "I don't need his money, Dad. Why would you *do* this?"

"It wasn't right that he wasn't helping. You make children, you look after them."

"Exactly. That's what I'm doing!"

"With my help. But I won't live forever," he added in a grumble. "I need to know you'll be all right after I'm gone."

Her heart sank. "Dad."

"Amelia." Hunter pinned her with his silver-bullet gaze as he came through a bed of petunias, trampling the pink and white and indigo trumpets. His unbuttoned jacket flared open to reveal his gray vest and amethyst tie.

Her heart lurched in a painfully bittersweet relief. She had been fairly convinced he was patching things up with Eden and the wedding would continue.

Maybe it would. She searched his granite features, but couldn't read what his pursuing her to the parking lot meant. As much as *The Runaway Groom* sounded like an uplifting rom-com, it was actually a nightmare to be the cause of something like this. She felt sick and guilty and very much the target of his resentment.

The man with the phone turned to catch Hunter's

approach and Hunter seemed to ignore him, but as he got close enough, he grabbed the phone and spun it back the way he'd come, sending the phone into the sea of petunias.

Oh. Amelia covered her mouth.

"Hey!" The man swore and ran toward the flower patch.

The people at the door began to squeal and laugh. Some of them were holding up their own phones, recording every second of this interchange.

"I have to take Dad home." This was worse than a nightmare. She moved to the door of her car. "My number hasn't changed. Reach out when you're ready to talk."

"I'm ready right now."

"I'll go finish my drink," her father said.

"Don't you dare," Amelia hissed.

Hunter intercepted Tobias and shot out his hand. "Hunter Waverly. I appreciate you coming today. This was important. Something I needed to hear."

"Tobias Lindor." He shook Hunter's hand. "Yes. You did. You two take as long as you need."

"We will, but not here."

"Pfft." Damned right she wasn't staying here. Not one second longer.

But as she opened the back door, intending to strap Peyton into her seat, Hunter leaned into the front from the passenger side. He turned off the car and stole the keys, straightening to hand them to her father.

"Stay as long as you like. They'll start serving food soon."

"What are you doing?" She popped out again, still holding Peyton as she scowled across the roof. "Dad doesn't drive." Only on the streets he knew, because of his bad eye. Not at all if he'd been drinking.

"I'll work something out," her father insisted, pocketing the keys and walking back to the tasting room.

Men.

"I'm not going anywhere with you." She had to lean in to talk to Hunter across the back seat where he had begun to fiddle with Peyton's seat. "Leave that alone."

"We can't talk here." He paused to remove his jacket, revealing perspiration stains on his shirt, perhaps not as impervious to all of this as he seemed.

"We don't have to talk *now*," she said with exasperation, switching Peyton's weight to her other arm. "This isn't a national emergency. We can both take a beat and process, can't we? I'll have my people call your people." After she found people.

"I would love nothing else." His tone was weary and patronizing. He yanked the seat out, slammed the door and came around to her side, forcing her to straighten and face him. "But look around."

The one man was still feeling around in the petunias, searching for his phone, but everyone else had fanned out to record them. They were keeping their distance, but it was still disgusting.

"I don't want strangers taking photos of my baby." She cradled Peyton closer.

"Neither do I. That's why we're leaving. Do you need that?" He pointed at the diaper bag on the seat.

"Yes, but—" She didn't want to be railroaded.

She didn't want to become an online meme, either.

"Here's Denis." Hunter retrieved her bag and slammed the car door, then he opened her driver door, pressed the lock button and slammed that, too.

An SUV stopped behind her car and a wiry, middle-aged man leaped out, leaving it running as he efficiently installed the car seat with a click and a smile.

Conflicted, Amelia climbed into a deliciously cool and roomy back seat. She buckled Peyton in, tucked her blankie around her, then clicked her own belt, blowing a stray tendril of hair from her eyes.

It will be okay, she assured herself, even though her stomach was churning with misgiving.

Maybe she could have believed it if Hunter hadn't looked so remote and menacing. Rather than take the passenger seat up front, he took the spot on the far side of Peyton. His tanned face was like carved and polished maple. Smooth, but hard.

"Where to, sir?" Denis asked as he wound his way out through the parking lot toward the exit.

"Goderich," Amelia said while Hunter spoke over her.

"The apartment." Hunter frowned at her. "It's in Toronto. Closer."

"It's kidnapping," she pointed out.

"Only if I ask for a ransom." He was texting as he spoke. "What kind of security do you have in Goderich?"

A dead bolt and venetian blinds.

"Why? Those people won't bother me in my own home, will they?" She twisted to look out the back window. A car was following them.

"In my experience, those sorts of people will climb on a trash can and photograph you on the toilet if they think they can earn a buck for it."

"Then why did you invite them to your wedding?"

"I didn't. This wasn't the easiest place to secure. *You* got in."

Ouch. But... "Is this some of the 'everything' you can give Peyton?" she asked with facetious bite. "You're right. I should have told you sooner."

"This will go more smoothly if we stick to what needs to happen rather than what has already happened. Yes, I'm here." He gave his attention to whoever he had just called.

He was talking to a group, Amelia realized as he began listing out assignments.

"Zudora, I need a paternity test. Have a nurse meet us at the apartment. Kimi, get everything a two-month-old needs. Leave it in one of the guest rooms. Who has the number for the wedding planner? Let her know that Denis will come back for Amelia's father and will arrange for his car to follow, but find him a hotel room if he prefers to stay the night. Carina, let me hear what you've got so far. No, don't say that."

"Say what?" Amelia prompted. She would really love to know what the heck was going on. Had his wedding been called off or merely postponed?

She didn't ask, not sure she was ready for the answer.

"No. Call it a brief relationship that ended before I met Eden. I want it to be clear I wasn't involved with her at any time while I was dating Eden."

Amelia's breath was punched out of her by that. She blocked out the rest and turned her face to the window.

She had no reason to be surprised or offended, she reminded herself. He had warned her not to come to his room if she expected it to go beyond that night.

"Tonight is enough," she had said, believing it in the moment. She had believed a lot of silly things that evening—that he respected her as a person, rather than seeing her as an object of entertainment. That he was rich, but grounded. That they had a connection that went beyond physical.

All of that delusion had been on her side. Worse, the infuriating awareness of him was still tingling and alive within her, making her feel his presence like a force that both pushed and pulled against her. Magnetism? Was that what it was?

It was agonizing and juvenile, and it was what had made her agree when Cheryl had said with excitement, "Table Fourteen invited us for drinks after we cash out."

The management had frowned on servers fraternizing with customers, but they didn't forbid it. Even so, Amelia usually kept things simple. She knew players when she saw them. She'd been involved with one already, and it hadn't ended well. A pair of men in upscale golf clothes with gold watches and aviator sunglasses were *not* looking for love. Besides, while one of them had a sexy French accent and a slow, lazy smile, the other was contained and remote and intimidating. Amelia had learned to gravitate toward golden retriever types, not men with energy that was brooding and coiled and dangerous.

"They probably have wives to get home to," Amelia had said, even as reluctant interest had been unfurling inside her.

"Don't you recognize them? That's Hunter Waverly. Wave-Com? And Remy Sylvain. Can-Carib airlines. I would do anything for a private flight to Turks and Caicos." Cheryl had waggled her brows.

Cheryl would do anything for a laugh and a pleasant roll in the hay. She had broken up with a long-term boyfriend and was determined to sow her oats before settling down again.

Amelia was the opposite. Her one serious relationship had left her wary and suffering a crisis of confidence. She'd been mad at men and had been hanging on to her virginity with stubborn defiance that had begun to feel like martyrdom—especially when an order took her past the men's table on the patio and she caught Hunter checking out her legs.

In that moment, she had seemed to walk from a gloomy fog into a bright, verdant day. A sharp sensation had pierced her, like a hunger pang, but lower. Her skin had warmed, and her heart had been in her throat that she had caught his interest.

It's only one drink. That was another thing she had allowed herself to believe. One drink was harmless. She hadn't already been in bed with him, mentally, before she'd given him her name.

Which was what made the whole thing so cringey. That's why she'd been glad to never see him again. He hadn't even had to seduce her. With nearly no effort at all, she had offered herself up. Here. Take me. Take my *virginity.*

Do you need money?

She would have buried her face in her hands, but Peyton began to whimper.

"You're okay, baby. It won't be long," she murmured and set her hand on Peyton's round belly.

It didn't work. Nothing did.

As Peyton worked herself up, Hunter stopped speaking to send them a distracted frown. "Is she okay?"

"She doesn't like long car rides." Amelia shrugged, defensive, but also passive-aggressively smug that Peyton was turning into a pill. Babies fussed. Figuring out why and solving it was Parenting 101. If he couldn't handle that, he should walk away from the gig right now.

"It might get loud here," he said to his minions. "See what you can get done. I'll check in when I get to the apartment." He ended his call.

Amelia tried to coax Peyton to take the pacifier, which she never took, but this time she sucked long enough for Amelia to ask, "Are you, um, still getting married?"

"You didn't notice the marquise-shaped dent in my face?"

She had forgotten he had that talent for arid remarks. She bit her lip, refusing to be amused. Or blamed. Or relieved.

Peyton spat out her pacifier and began to wail. Amelia gathered her patience and tried again, but Peyton turned her head in rejection.

"Are you seeing anyone?" Hunter asked.

"With this as my profile?" She waved at the growing tantrum Peyton was staging. "They're lined up out the door. Why?" Amelia barely heard him over their daughter, but a blush of hopefulness rose across her chest.

"Because this mess is big enough with just the two of you."

And that was the real reason she hadn't told him about Peyton. He didn't want either of them.

"No." She ignored the scorch in her throat that strained her voice, compelled to defend her daughter. "The two of *us*—" Amelia pointed between herself and Hunter "—made her. And she is not a mess. My life is not where I thought it would be, either, you know."

She might have pulled off that moment of righteousness if she didn't look like a carton of eggs dropped on the sidewalk and their daughter hadn't drowned her out by arriving at full nuclear meltdown.

"Is there something I can do?" Hunter asked impassively.

"No," she mumbled, wanting to fold over Peyton and cry just as hard.

Because this was a mess. It was a giant awful mess, and she couldn't help feeling it was all her fault.

CHAPTER FOUR

"STILL THINK BRINGING us here was a good idea?" Amelia taunted under her breath as she unclipped the car seat and allowed Hunter to lift it out the other side.

He wouldn't pretend the last hour hadn't been an exercise in endurance. Talking had become impossible. Peyton didn't like the car seat. She said so. Denis had put in his earbuds while Amelia had tried a dozen ways to soothe her. She had rubbed the silky border of the blanket on the baby's cheek and given her a snuggle toy and a pacifier, put socks on her feet and kissed her waving fists, but the infant had craned her neck and squirmed against her restraints and bellyached the whole way.

Hunter sympathized, strapped into his own inescapable situation.

The wedding had been off the minute Amelia appeared. He had resisted admitting it right up until he was walking into the Honeymoon Suite where Eden had waited for him, still in her gown. "It's bad luck to see the bride before the wedding," she had reminded him through semi-hysterical tears.

She had been prepared to go through with the wedding. They both needed their marriage and probably could have rescued the day. The interruption could have been spun into a farce and his surprise baby sold as a blessing. But after that?

After that, his daughter would have had a stepmother. As much as Hunter respected Eden and had been prepared to share parenting with her of whatever family they might have made together, he couldn't start Peyton's life that way. He couldn't start his own relationship with his child by bringing in another stranger, not that he spelled all of that out to Eden.

He had said the words. "We can't get married."

She had suggested postponing the wedding, but he rejected that, too. It had felt too much like postponing the inevitable, because there had been that other, shameful relief under his skin that he barely wanted to acknowledge.

It had become unpleasant at that point. "Quinn warned me not to marry you," Eden had spat hotly. "She said your family is addicted to scandal. She said you would take my ship down with yours. I chose to believe Vienna. I believed in you, Hunter."

That last remark had lashed deep across the place where he believed in himself. Where he knew himself to be a decent human being. Honorable. Not given to selfishness or callous behaviors that harmed others. *I'm doing this for my child*, he had wanted to assert, but to his chagrin, there was a grim gratification sitting in the pit of his belly. Amelia was back in his life and couldn't slip away so easily this time.

He loathed himself for being pleased by that. It was too much like his father. However, marrying Eden at the expense of what was right for Peyton would also be too much like Frank Waverly.

It was an untenable situation with no easy answer, making Peyton's screams of protest kind of cathartic while he brooded on the mistakes he'd made.

As if she understood that the shift of the carrier and the glimpse of blue sky between the skyscrapers meant freedom was imminent, she quieted, but her baby breaths were still catching.

God, she was tiny. If she didn't have this protective shell of a car seat and a handle that Hunter could grasp in a strong fist, he'd be terrified to hold her at all.

He waved off Denis and slipped the doorman a bill, asking him to order a late lunch for him and Amelia.

"You'll eat sushi?" he asked Amelia.

She nodded, slowing as they entered the lobby. She glanced from the security desk to the chandelier suspended three stories above, then to the spacious visitors' lounge with its silk rug and fresh floral arrangements and colorful aquarium built into the back wall.

When the elevator dinged, she hugged herself and ducked her head, hurrying to enter with him.

"Don't be like that," he said as he used his thumbprint to access his floor. "You knew who I was when we met." But it was hitting him that she wasn't someone like Eden or Vienna who took this level of comfort for granted.

"Is this, like, a company building or something?"

"I am the company." It was an exhausting truth and a reality that couldn't be changed. Especially not after he'd fought so hard for the privilege.

He felt her gaze lift to touch the side of his face. "What about Vienna?"

"She prefers that I vote her share." Neal had been after Vi to give him her proxy. Their stepmother had soured both of them on spousal involvement in the company, and Vi had always had other interests. She left the company to Hunter and always backed up his decisions, but the fact that she didn't trust her husband told Hunter all was not well with her marriage. Between their father's death, the court case and the wedding, however, Hunter hadn't had a chance to dig into it with her.

Now he had this—he looked at the baby—circumstance.

The doors slid open and Amelia said with great cheer, "Guess what, Peyton? You get to come out of your car seat!"

Hunter set the seat on the wide bench in the foyer and watched as Amelia released Peyton. If anything, some of her tension seemed to dissipate as she gathered up the baby and kissed her cheek. She closed her eyes and made a contented noise as she nuzzled the baby, behaving as though she had missed her daughter when the kid hadn't been out of her sight for a second.

It was cute, though, especially when Peyton let her head snuggle into Amelia's shoulder and opened her mouth against her own fist. All seemed right in her little world now, too.

Through a vague sense of being shut out, Hunter still had to acknowledge how beautiful they were, like a Renaissance painting with the baby's lashes drooping and light stealing in to frost the wisps of hair framing Amelia's face. She was wan, but her skin was clear and smooth, her mouth pink and somber. Angelic.

He had the urge to kiss her. Not in foreplay, but in greeting. Maybe foreplay, too. Despite only knowing her the one night, she had stayed in his thoughts along with a near constant ache of want. He wanted the right to touch her and kiss her when her eyes were closed and open his mouth across hers with more purpose—

Amelia's lashes lifted, and she caught him staring.

He looked away, annoyed with himself. This was battle conditions, not a time to let his libido cloud his judgment.

"We have a lot to discuss. We're losing our chance to control the narrative. Come." He led her into the lounge. "Do you want anything? Coffee? Something stronger?"

"I'm breastfeeding," she reminded. "I try to stay sober when I'm in charge of another life."

"Is that a dig?" Because as appealing as getting

blackout drunk sounded, he didn't usually have more than two or three himself. He was charged with the lives and livelihoods of thousands of workers. Also, his stepmother had covered the ground of public drunkenness pretty thoroughly. He didn't need to contribute anything to that cause.

"It's a fact," she murmured, wandering the open plan, taking in the Italian marble and twenty-foot ceiling and floating stairs to the upper floor. She paused to study the Casson and the Carmichael before moving to the wall of windows that stretched to the upper floor. Beyond was the spacious terrace, the city skyline and the horizon where the blurred line of Lake Ontario met cloudless sky.

"You play?" She nodded at the grand piano.

"Vienna does."

"She lives here, too?"

"She and Neal have a place on the waterfront that they use when they're in town."

"You bought this for you and Eden," she said in a tone of realization, tilting the engagement photo on the end table.

He had an urge to take it from her and throw it in a drawer. He would do that. Later.

"No, we're—" He swore as he remembered something and brought out his phone, texting his real estate agent to put a hold on the house in Bridle Path. "This is mine. It's a good location and convenient for entertaining." The kitchen noise was tucked behind closed doors, the big screen was a button-touch from descending from the ceiling, and the building was in the city center.

Amelia gave him a befuddled look. "You don't strike me as a partier."

"This doesn't scream raves and orgies?" He waved at himself, still in his tailored but very traditional morning suit. "I hold charity events and host those who expect it."

"Like?"

"Celebrities." He shrugged. "Athletes in town for a game. VIPs from overseas."

She tucked her chin. "That's the kind of people you invite for supper?"

"Sometimes." He shrugged it off, never starstruck. They were people. Some pleasant, others vapid. Either way, he didn't want to talk about them right now. "I'll start the coffee and get changed. I have decaf and soft drinks." He led her into the kitchen. "I usually have a housekeeper, but most of my regular staff were given the next two weeks off since I expected to be on my honeymoon."

She made a noise halfway between a choke and a cough, pausing at the autographed photo that hung inside the door to the kitchen. "I've seen him on the celebrity chef Bake-Off thing. He cooks for you?"

"He does the annual benefit for our foundation." He poured beans into the grinder and pushed the button, nearly missing what she said because of the noise.

"Of course he does," she snorted.

"Why is that funny?" he asked when the grinder silenced.

"It's not. Is that filter real gold?"

He turned from setting it and filled the carafe from the tap. "You're judging me."

"No."

She was, and it annoyed him. Was that why she hadn't told him he had a kid? Because she was a snob who disdained wealth? In case she hadn't noticed, she wasn't his first choice to share parenting, either.

"I'll make a call, find out when the nurse is supposed to get here." He glanced at the clock. "The paternity test will inform a lot of our decisions." He finished filling the coffee maker, swiveled the filter into place and pressed the button. "Here." He opened the refrigerator and waved at the door. "See if there's something you might like."

She turned the labels on the soda bottles. "Lime and jasmine, rhubarb and cardamom, fennel…" She gave her head a shake. "I didn't even know these flavors exist."

"Try the cola with pear. It's good. Actually, it probably has caffeine. There are organic juices, too."

"Can I, um, use the washroom?"

"Sure. It's through there." He pointed.

"Thanks." She offered Peyton.

For two thudding heartbeats, his brain couldn't make sense of what she was doing. Then a bolt of realization struck him. He took the baby, stomach pitching because holding her was like trying to cradle a soap bubble without popping it.

Amelia walked away, and he swallowed a reflexive, *Wait. Come back. What do I do?*

Hunter knew to protect her neck, but that was where his familiarity with babies ended. What else were you supposed to do? Feed 'em and clean 'em and keep them from being eaten by wild animals, he supposed.

This felt a lot like holding a freshly caught fish, given her absent wiggling. The average salmon weighed more than she did, though, and they didn't have delicate limbs that looked like they could snap in a stiff breeze.

Her wandering gaze found his, and she smiled.

Why that hit him like a kick in his chest, he couldn't say. Maybe because that dimple high on her cheek was exactly like Vi's. Maybe it was her oblivious joy. Her unconditional welcome at finding someone new. That smile of hers was so happy and pure it hurt to see, like looking into the sun.

Maybe it hurt because this was the moment he'd been avoiding. Holding her and seeing her forced him to acknowledge her. She was his. He didn't need a test. He would do his due diligence, but too many things pointed to the obvious. He had made this child with Amelia.

With acknowledgment came the repercussions, all deeper than he'd been prepared to face until he had to. Here they came, though. Even as he smirked back, guilt washed through him because Amelia was right. Peyton *had* been better off not knowing she was a Waverly. His name would impact her from now until the end of time, and all the five-star meals and chartered planes in the world couldn't protect her from it.

His arms instinctually enfolded her in apology and a desire to protect.

As her achingly delicate weight met the wall of his chest, his heart slammed hard enough he feared he might bruise her, but his arms contracted, holding her closer still.

What the hell was happening to him? A ferocious strength was gathering in him, the kind that would step in front of a charging grizzly to protect her. At the same time, he felt so damned vulnerable a cold sweat lifted on his skin.

A few hours ago, he hadn't even known he had created this life, but he was suddenly sick with the knowledge that life would happen to her. She would fall off swing sets and get her feelings hurt by some jerk at school. She would have a fender bender and go on spring break to Florida and face sexism and fall in love only to have her heart broken. Those bumps were inevitable, and he already couldn't forgive himself for letting them happen to her.

She gurgled and wiggled and batted her fist against his Adam's apple, gently hammering herself into his heart and blood and soul.

She took all the labels he had applied to himself through the years—son, brother, friend, man, CEO... Today, he had even been prepared to call himself a husband.

He had never once imagined the power and humility in calling himself a *father*.

He swallowed, shaken to realize he had been re-acting as he did to any iceberg strike against his ship. Contain the damage, deploy a team, salvage what was valuable. Recover.

Recovery wasn't possible. That hard truth im-pacted him like a brain-jarring uppercut. Peyton wasn't a scandal to be contained. She wasn't chang-ing his life. She was changing him. *He* had to rise to this new role and rethink all his objectives, be-cause his child had just become his top priority. His next steps weren't about spinning what had happened today. They were about shaping his future and en-suring that future held plenty of room for Peyton.

And therefore Amelia.

A sensation like a shot of whiskey went straight to his gut and radiated into his pelvis.

He turned his thoughts from where they had au-tomatically gone. Did he want to sleep with Amelia again? Sure. On a base, randy level, of course.

Sex would complicate an already complex rela-tionship, he reminded himself, trying to cool his jets. They would share custody and he would have to make Toronto his home base so he could be more accessible to his daughter—

Unless…

He absently rubbed Peyton's back, trying to be objective about the thought that had popped into his head. Was he *trying* to completely level his life? Be-cause a traditional wedding to someone like Eden had made sense. A spur-of-the-moment marriage to Amelia would come across as a wild impulse driven by the sort of horny passion that had motivated his father's marriage to Irina.

Or it could be the spin that saved him from looking like a philanderer who preyed on hapless waitresses. From a practical point, moving Amelia and Peyton into his home would provide both of them the most security possible.

He would need a watertight prenup, obviously. For Peyton's sake, they would have to make an honest effort at a real, successful marriage.

He ignored the fresh spark of heat that kindled in his lap. That's not why he would propose. He was warming to the idea in other ways, though. It solved a lot of issues very neatly.

"Thanks," Amelia said in a subdued voice, returning with dampness around her hairline. She came across and held out her hands.

Still raw and self-conscious at how thoroughly Peyton had reconfigured his view of himself, he gave up the baby and watched Peyton brighten and grin. She knew her mama, and it caused the envy bug to nip into Hunter. He wanted his child to react to him like that. Which meant becoming a part of her daily life.

Amelia's expression softened briefly, but when she transferred her attention to him, she sobered, and her tone became resolved.

"I've decided to go to my cousin's."

CHAPTER FIVE

ONE OF HUNTER's dark brows pulled down and in. Not in an aggressive or angry way. More an indication that he was concentrating or trying to solve a puzzle. It was as though he were studying the behavior of an animal that didn't make sense to him.

"This is too much," she expounded.

He lived in a two-story mansion in the top of Toronto's most expensive building. The toilet lid had lifted as she entered the powder room, for heaven's sake. The seat warmed itself. He had bought out a vineyard and owned real art. Not cheap prints, but actual originals by famous dead people.

No wonder he had set a one-night limit when he invited her into his room at that B and B. No wonder he had never tried to call her and had brushed her off so unceremoniously when she reached out to him. Bringing her here wasn't about trying to "protect" her and Peyton. He was *hiding* them. He was trying to protect himself and this lifestyle of his.

"You and Dad are making decisions for me that aren't yours to make," she added, resenting it all over again. She kept thinking, *If I had just said no, if I had insisted on going to yoga, none of this would have happened.* Her father would have been forced to tell her what he wanted to do and none of this would have happened.

Hunter's lips parted as though he was about to say something.

"This isn't fair. It's not *right*." She hurried to talk over him, but she was distracted by his mouth. She had forgotten how full his bottom lip was. It was wide and undeniably masculine. Powerfully sexy. Everything about him was screaming superiority and affluence and seductive appeal, from his clean-shaven jaw to his shiny shoes. It was disconcerting. Intimidating.

His natural air of authority tempted her to trust him and let him take over, which scared her. This baby they'd made had already consumed her life, and Peyton had come about because Amelia allowed herself to leap into a brief infatuation. At least when Hunter had offered one night and that's all she'd given him, it had been an even exchange.

Today she was seeing the endless resources he had at his disposal. Independence was one of the few she had left, so she was exercising it.

"You can't take over my life," she insisted, even as she felt as though she was talking to a cat. A big, dangerous jungle cat that only noticed her because she was making noise. He was flicking his tail with boredom, letting her chatter and squawk because he wasn't hungry yet, but he had the weight of his paw on her, making it impossible to get away. "We share a baby, but we can work out how to share her in a way that doesn't involve you keeping me here like some prisoner in a tower."

His chin dipped in the barest hint of *You think not?*

"My cousin's husband works in Parliament. He'll know how to handle reporters and keep photographers off the lawn."

Hunter only brought out his phone and dialed, setting it to speaker when someone named Carina answered.

"Status update," he prompted.

"They're calling my flight. One sec." Presumably, Carina found a place to speak where she wouldn't be overheard. When she came back on the line, her tone was hushed and rushed, pulling no punches. "It's trending. Obviously, there's been a race for scoops by the online editions. The general tone is that Eden is a victim, you're a cad, Amelia is the other woman."

Amelia's mouth fell open with affront.

Hunter touched his lips and nodded, indicating she should stay quiet and listen.

"Eden has put out a brief statement confirming the wedding was called off. We've requested she coordinate a more detailed statement with our team, but we'll see if she complies. We have also confirmed the wedding is off, making no comment on the baby rumors. We're promising further information in due course and have requested privacy at this time. We'll know better on Monday how this affects stock prices.

The anticipation is a drop of six points. There's an emerging narrative that the Waverly scandals are more of a family-wide issue, not just Irina, so recovering stock value could take time. Most of the directors were at the wedding. Did you talk to any of them? Some are asking for an emergency meeting."

"I know who's asking," Hunter said. "Put that off at least a week so stock price can level."

"Will do. The nurse should arrive within the hour. How confident are you that the baby is yours? Vienna had the idea for your grandparents to take Amelia's father to their cottage."

"Confident," he stated, holding Amelia's gaze so unwaveringly, her breath halted in her lungs. "They should do that and plan to stay at least a week, likely two."

"Done. When can I sit with Amelia? We need everything they might dig up on her family so we can get ahead of it. And photos. The ones from the winery are making it too easy for attack. Once we're on an apology tour, we'll get family photos and a feature, but right now I suggest staging something for paparazzi that shows her being a protective mom and you being the helpful dad."

Amelia recoiled, unable to find adequate words to express her outrage and disgust.

"See if Vienna's stylist is available," Hunter said. "If not, find someone and come straight here when you land. See if one of the visitor units is open so you can stay in the building."

"Will do. Final call for boarding. See you soon."

He ended the call, brows lifting in a very annoying, supercilious way.

"Carina was also on vacation, visiting family in Nova Scotia."

"Now it's my fault her vacation has been interrupted?"

"I'm saying it would be rude if you decided not to be here when she's on her way to meet with you."

"Like I have a choice!" she cried, becoming teary as she heard again, *Amelia is the other woman*.

"You always have a choice," he said in a tone that sounded patronizing. Pitying. "You can leave if you insist, but until I know otherwise, Peyton is my daughter. Therefore, it's incumbent on me to protect her. If your leaving puts her in danger—"

"Don't you dare threaten me," she warned, insides beginning to quake.

"It's not a threat. It's reality. This is what we're up against." He indicated his phone and everything Carina had revealed. "Let me protect both of you."

She refused to believe her life was spiraling this far out of her control. Surely Carina was exaggerating?

"Where's the diaper bag?" she asked, looking to the door to the lounge.

"You should find everything you need for Peyton upstairs."

"I want my phone."

"To confirm what's being said?" He shook his head gravely. "That wouldn't be productive, Amelia."

She held his stare while pressure built in her chest

and throat and behind her eyes. *I'll do what I want. You're not the boss of me. This doesn't have to happen this way.*

"This is all your fault!" she blurted childishly.

"And I'm taking responsibility."

"Oh—!" She spun and hurried back to the foyer where she hovered her hand over the bag, then snatched it up before starting up the stairs.

Peyton was overdue for a change and was still wearing the short-sleeved onesie Amelia had put her in this morning. Here in this air-conditioned palace, she needed warmer clothes.

At the top of the stairs, Amelia glanced in the first open door and found a tastefully decorated guest room brimming with deliveries. Boxes and shopping bags were spilling out of the floor of the closet. Clothes in infant sizes hung from the rail. A playpen was set up in the corner and next to it stood a high-end changing table with a bumper around its padded top. Its shelves were stocked with diapers and creams and wet wipes—all the organic, biodegradable, skin-sensitive brands. *Big spender.*

She pulled a cotton sleeper from her diaper bag and placed Peyton on the table.

Hunter leaned in the doorway. His long jacket was abandoned somewhere, but he still wore his snug vest and tailored trousers. The suit emphasized the power in his shoulders and wide chest. His shirt strained against his biceps as he folded his arms.

"You're just going to stand there and continue to intimidate me?" Amelia asked.

"Is that what I'm doing? I thought I was observing a caretaking procedure."

"You want to learn how to change her?"

"So I can evaluate the nanny's competence once I hire one, yes."

"I look after her myself. If you're not prepared to do that, why would I grant you any access at all?" she asked with peevish superiority.

"It was a joke." He came to stand on the pedal of the waste basket, holding the lid open for her. "And, look. You're allowed to be angry."

"Gosh, thanks." The wet diaper landed with a dull thud in the bottom of the can.

"But it doesn't change anything. I'm furious, too," he said in a tone that was almost conversational. *Nice weather, eh?*

Behind his eyes, however, there was a flash of incendiary fury that made her suck in a breath that burned.

"Gaining custody and the right to provide for her is something I *have* to do," he said in an implacable tone. His pensive look skimmed her face, then shifted to Peyton. "It's not performative. I didn't arrive here the way I thought I would, but I've always known what kind of father I wanted to be."

Amelia's pulse skipped, and she paused in securing the fresh diaper. "What kind is that?"

"Present," he said flatly. "One who does the right thing. One who protects his child instead of putting his own whims and desires first."

Her umbrage against him eased a notch. She tried

to remember what she knew of his family, but it wasn't much. His father had died a few years ago and there'd been a drawn-out court battle with his stepmother over control of Wave-Com. He'd been in the middle of that when they'd met, not that he had talked about it. Remy had made some remark about the golf weekend being necessary to help his friend unwind, though.

In the weeks after, Amelia had been consumed by her search for Jasper. She hadn't followed the twists and turns of Hunter's journey to legal triumph. By the time she realized she was pregnant with his baby, he was out of the headlines and she was turning inward with grief.

To her mind, though, all of those things reported on TV had happened to someone else, not the Hunter Waverly she knew. The man she had slept with had been surprisingly human while the one on TV was a mythical legend from a dynastic family. That one had wealth and power and little empathy for mere mortals like her.

That was the one who confronted her today. He had no compunction about sweeping her into his world and mercilessly making her face how impossible it was for her to go back to the life she knew and loved. He was so armed and armored, she couldn't touch him.

But for a second, one tiny second, she saw the man who had held her hand and called her amazing and made her feel incredible things.

She blinked, and he was turning away.

"I'll change and meet you downstairs. Our lunch will be here any minute."

"You said you liked sushi." Hunter's voice broke into Amelia's introspection. "Do you prefer a fork? I'm not a purist."

"Pardon? Oh." She adjusted her grip on her chopsticks and blinked at the array of seafood before them. While she had taken a couple of rolls, Hunter had polished off half the platter and most of the teriyaki chicken and seemed to be eyeing the last of the yam tempura, which she had yet to taste.

"I'm not very hungry." She glanced to where Peyton had just kicked a jangling toy on the play gym arched over where she lay on an activity mat.

What was she going to do? Things were so much worse than she had feared.

"You looked," Hunter said with heavy disappointment. "Didn't you?"

"What?" She flashed her gaze back to his, then dropped it guiltily.

This was what she got for searching his name online. She had only wanted to know more about his father and stepmother, but that hadn't come to the top of the page. Her own name had. Apparently, she was ruining Eden Bellamy's life.

The Bellamy family was considered a national treasure. Amelia knew that, so maybe she should have been prepared to be vilified, but it wasn't as if she had done this on purpose! Her baby was completely innocent in all of this, yet there had been some very sickening things said about Peyton as well. Things awful enough to make her want to cry.

"They're trolls, Amelia. Not worth thinking about."

"But I had messages from friends. They want to know what's going on and why I never told them you were Peyton's father."

"What did you say?" His words came out fast and crisp enough to lash like a whip.

"Nothing. I don't know what to say. Other than mind your own beeswax," she added in a grumble.

He let out an exhale. "That's why we're bringing in a team. They'll clean up your timeline and craft stock answers to the most awkward questions. You'll feel back in control very soon."

"Will I?" she scoffed. "Or will you? Because if you're going to tell me what to say, that's not really me in control, is it?"

"This is a very big bus, Amelia. I already know how to drive it. I won't ask you to lie, only stay on message."

She snorted and picked up a round of BC roll, swirling it in soy sauce and wasabi before popping the morsel of barbecued salmon and cucumber in her mouth. She chewed and swallowed, chasing it with a salty sip of her miso soup.

"I'm predisposed to hate PR people," she explained once she'd swallowed. "The company that sent Jasper to Chile did everything they could to quiet his disappearance. It made them look bad. I would sit with a reporter for hours, pouring my guts out, hoping to get some attention and support. The story would be watered down or outright killed before it posted. If I got a government official to take an interest, they would suddenly ghost me and I'd be back to square one. I can't prove it, but I know his employers were behind the obstruction. I realize people like Carina are a necessary evil for you, but to me they're just evil."

"Understood." His cheeks went hollow. He had changed into cream-colored pants and a checked shirt. The short sleeves were rolled up once, revealing more of his tanned upper arms. "For me, they've always been more necessary than evil. My life has been one publicity nightmare after another since my mother died."

That's what Amelia had wanted to learn more about. She stopped chasing a clump of rice and gave him her full attention.

"I remember the odd headline about a wardrobe malfunction and some Twitter feuds. Were there other issues?" she asked.

"So many," he said with disgust. "You can still find a lot of them online if you look hard enough, even the affairs."

"She cheated on your father?"

"I don't know if it can be called cheating if he knew about it and put up with it. Maybe it was her kink to step out, and he got off on being cuckolded. It's none of my business if that's the case, but she slept with married men when Dad was in the middle of cutting deals with them. Their wives would find out and everything would go to hell, so it affected the company. That *is* my business." He tapped his chest.

"Because you knew the company was coming to you? Or were you working there by then?"

"Both. I barely remember a time when I wasn't getting a paycheck from Wave-Com. Even before Mom died, Dad would pick us up from school and take us back to the office. We were sitting through high-level meetings before we had our times tables memorized."

"That sounds like he was at least trying to connect with you and your sister."

"In his way, maybe. Once Mom was gone and he was married to Irina, going to the office was the only way I could see him without her there. I was fourteen when the first board member came to me, complaining about her and asking me to 'talk to' my old man."

"That's a terrible thing to ask of a kid."

"It was, but someone had to. It helped me in the long run. I had relationships with all of them. They backed me when Irina tried to take control of Wave-Com after Dad died."

"Did she really think she had a chance? Did she have experience?"

"God, no. But ignorance of little things like the law never stopped her from doing what she wanted. At one point, she decided she didn't have to pay her maid. Dad didn't find out until the human rights tribunal got involved."

"Oh, *no*."

"Oh, yes. She did childish, tacky things, too. When

Vi got married, Irina had a penis cake brought out instead of the wedding cake. She thought it would be funny. She was always doing things like that. If there was an occasion where one of us was being celebrated, she had to bring us down a peg and grab the spotlight for herself. Today, when your dad showed up, I honestly thought for a minute that she'd hired him, purely to embarrass me."

"Really?" Amelia lost her grip on her chopsticks. They skewed, sending the round she held rolling off the edge of her plate.

"Really." He caught it with his fingers and ate it.

"Does she have mental health issues? Trouble processing appropriate behavior?"

"Perhaps." He shrugged. "That's no excuse for being mean. And greedy. And criminally irresponsible. She has never tried to curb her own behavior. Trying to help her was a no-win situation. If anything, she enjoys the control of inciting chaos. Of making others fix whatever she breaks."

"Why didn't your father divorce her?"

"Great question. *He didn't want to.*" Hunter's rage was so cold and condensed, his clothing should have frozen and shattered, dropping off his body. "I genuinely don't know what he saw in her. Can anyone be that good in bed that you would let them humiliate your kids on a regular basis?"

An acute pain stabbed in the middle of her chest. "I'm so sorry, Hunter."

"It's nothing to do with you," he dismissed brusquely. "Thankfully our grandparents—the ones who are taking your father to Lake of the Woods—took us as often as they could. They're my mother's parents. Prairie folk. Steady as you get. And Irina is in Palm Springs now, married to some other unfortunate twit. You don't have to worry about her."

"No, I mean I'm sorry for today. Like, really sorry." So sorry, she felt sick. "You must hate us."

"No." Shadows shifted behind his eyes. "But don't do it again." There was no levity in his flat order. He meant it.

Peyton started to fuss, allowing Amelia to escape the intensity of his hard stare.

Peyton immediately began to root, so Amelia brought the receiving blanket with her and sat back at the table, settling Peyton to nurse before she picked up her chopsticks again. Her stomach was still in remorseful knots.

"The truth is, I was glad when you brushed off my text," she admitted. "I didn't know how to face you. I felt stupid for getting pregnant." She had felt like a cliché. Who got pregnant on their first time in this day and age? "I thought you'd be angry, or think I did it on purpose, and I was grieving Jasper so hard." Her eyes stung and her chest burned whenever she talked about him, but she pushed on. "I didn't have the energy to work out custody. I *needed* her to be mine." She cradled Peyton closer and breathed through the ache that sat like a knife in her breastbone. "But if I had known you would find out like this, I would have come to you sooner."

"I believe you." He nodded, but a small spasm

flickered across his face. His voice became gruff. "Thank you. I would have loved for Irina to apologize just once. To mean it."

"I do."

"I know." He looked to the window and flicked his hand with weariness. "I make it a policy not to apologize for Irina's history because it implies I'm responsible for her behavior, but I realize her notoriety colors all of this, making it that much more difficult for you."

"Why couldn't you just be the guy at the hardware store?" she said, but bit her lip. He was probably thinking *Why couldn't you be rich and influential like me?* "I will play ball with your PR people," she assured him. "We can do photos or whatever, so you look like a helpful dad. I realize it's in Peyton's best interest."

"Amelia." Her name was tinged with exasperation. "I intend to *be* a helpful dad. *That's* in her best interest."

"Nanny remark notwithstanding?"

He didn't crack a smile. He ran his tongue over his teeth behind his lip, watching her and seeming to consider his words. He picked up his coffee and sipped, then stared into it.

"My marriage to Eden was supposed to demonstrate that I wasn't like my father. That I'm a steady man who is a paragon of family values."

She sat back. "Do you hear how cold that sounds? Weren't you marrying because you love each other?"

"We like each other. Past tense on her part, I imagine." His mouth curled with self-deprecation. "But our marriage made sense in concrete ways. You're judging me again." His eyes narrowed. "There were sound business reasons, and we were both ready to start a family. Arranged marriage is not forced marriage. You feel a lot more comfortable merging fortunes if it will go to children you make together."

"It's none of my business." She tried to sound as though she meant it. Believed it. "I just wouldn't sign up for a loveless marriage myself. That's all."

"No?" His tone had the precision of a scalpel. "Because it's an effective way to address needs that go beyond romantic delusions."

"Excuse me," she huffed. "If you weren't in love with Eden, that's fine. In fact, I'm glad." A little too glad. "It means you won't blame me for your broken heart, but love isn't a delusion."

"That kind isn't," he said, waving at the blanket.

Peyton had fallen asleep, so Amelia anchored the blanket with her chin and wrangled to cover herself while trying not to wake her daughter.

"But what did you tell me last year?" Hunter challenged lightly. "That you had recently broken up after a long relationship. You thought you loved him, but you were wrong. Delusion."

"That was a very specific case." Of a man who had led her on because he was trying to get her into bed. When she had asked him to wait, he had cheated on her. She didn't like revisiting her naivete, and she didn't appreciate having her words thrown back in her face.

She loosely wrapped the blanket around Peyton and adjusted the infant's position on her bent arm.

"I'll take her so you can eat." He rose, and Amelia was too bemused to protest as Hunter picked her up. He was careful not to wake her, and he made sure the blanket was smooth, not bunched beneath her.

He looked surprisingly confident, as though he had been settling Peyton in the crook of his arm since the day she was born. There was even a ruefulness in his gaze as he sat and looked at his daughter in a way that made Amelia's heart swoop.

She picked up her chopsticks and shoved a bite in her mouth, but couldn't swallow past the lump in her throat. In her heart of hearts, she had wanted him to look at Peyton that way, but witnessing it was too much to bear. It sparked a panicked sense of threat in her, forcing her to face that they *would* share custody. She already begrudged him the time she would miss with her daughter.

"What is your vision of marriage? Fall in love with the guy from the hardware store and hope it works out?"

"What's wrong with wanting to fall for a decent guy with a decent job? My mom worked at the sewing store and fell for the guy from the salt mine. They…" She shrugged, growing teary again because it had seemed like a very simple, common dream that should be attainable by anyone, but it had eventually turned to ash. Now it seemed further beyond her reach than ever. "They were very happy, and I always thought I would have what they had. The house wasn't fancy and our cars were always used and practical. There were tough times when interest rates went up and Dad was laid off, but it was a very loving home. My brother was my best friend, and he made me boxed mac and cheese when Mom had to work late. Dad taught me to ride a bike and built us a tree house."

"That's what you want for Peyton?"

"Now who's judging?" She lifted her chin, but after a moment, her spine softened and she found herself drawing patterns in a smear of soy sauce with the tips of her chopsticks. "It was what I wanted when I was growing up. I wanted to be a teacher so I could have summers off with my kids. Mom would take them on weekends so I could go on date nights with my husband. She would make cookies and Uncle Jasper would take them fishing with Dad."

Don't. Cry.

She sat up straight and took a big gulp of cold water.

"I can still have pieces of that," she reminded herself. "Maybe I'll still fall for the hardware guy. Maybe he'll already have a child of his own. Hopefully Peyton will be as close to his kids as I was to Jasper. It's not a lost dream, just a different one, but I'm not ready to think about it, so I don't."

"I don't want that."

"Yes, I know. I saw what you want." God, Eden was so beautiful. Everything about that wedding had been first class. They would have had their whole lifetime planned, from skiing in Europe to going on African safaris over spring break. Their children would have gone to all the top schools, starting in preschool all the way to the best university. Then they would marry another elite like they were and the legacy would continue.

"No." His features grew craggy with tension. "I don't want her to have a stepfather. I want her to have *me*."

She opened her mouth, made herself pause and grasp at her patience, but there really was a limit to how much of her life she would let him dictate.

"I can see why stepparents would be a sore spot for you. I get it. I do. Plus, you're only starting to bond with her so you don't want me dating anyone and messing with that. I'm not planning to. If I did, I would wait ages before introducing them to her and I swear I would let you meet them first, so quit feeling threatened."

"No. Amelia." His smile was so patronizing she wanted to roll her eyes. "I want her to have both of us. In the same house. We can give her as many brothers and sisters as you want."

"I—" She scratched her brow, genuinely lost because he couldn't be suggesting what she thought he was suggesting. "What?"

"I want us to marry."

"No," she said reflexively.

"Think about it."

"No."

There was a ring of some internal bell.

"The nurse is here." He rose and walked away while Amelia kept thinking, *No.*

CHAPTER SIX

THE TEST WAS a cheek swab that Peyton slept through. Hunter gave his own sample and showed the nurse to the door.

"I'll put her down and have a shower if you don't mind," Amelia said, still cradling the sleeping baby.

She was trying to avoid him and the proposition he'd put forth. Hunter could tell. Was she disappointed he hadn't been more romantic about it? The hardware guy would have gone down on one knee and offered a diamond worth two months of his salary, he was sure, but what did that prove?

Their marrying made sense. He wanted to keep talking until she saw that, which was how he behaved in most business negotiations, but Amelia's hollow cheeks suggested she was on her last nerve. He would have to give her a little time to process and come around to seeing the wisdom in it herself.

"Do you want something clean to wear? I think Vi left a dress here that might fit you." He waved her to precede him up the stairs.

"*Vi* did," Amelia said skeptically.

He bit back a sigh, not used to being disbelieved or having to make explanations for himself, but he could understand her suspicion that it belonged to Eden.

"Vienna was shopping and brought it up when she came for lunch. She wanted to try it on again because she thought she might return it, then she forgot it in the foyer. I left it upstairs for whenever she comes by again." He veered into the other guest room to fetch the flat box with the embossed scroll of the boutique's name.

When he came back to the room full of baby gear, Amelia was reading the back of an unopened baby monitor. Peyton was in the playpen, fast asleep, wrapped in a duck-print blanket snug as a tortilla around a burrito.

"I can figure out the monitor," Hunter said, setting the box on the bed. "Helpful dad, remember?"

"This isn't a reality show. I'm not going to marry you for TV ratings." She handed him the monitor, though, and lifted the top off the box, peering at the dress.

"I'm not trying to portray myself as a better father than my own. I want to *be* better. You would still get a decent guy with a decent job." Actually, his position was demanding as hell, but it had its perks—designer dresses like that, for instance. "Auntie Vienna will make cookies with her niece," he added with a nod to Peyton. "Actually, they'll probably finger paint. I realize that's not the same, but it's something. Uncle Remy would love to take her fishing with your

dad." In Martinique. Was she open to outright brib-
ery? Because he could go on.

"We don't even know each other. You didn't want
to get to know me," she reminded him as bright red
spots arrived on her cheekbones. Her voice quavered
with degradation as she added, "It was a one-night
hookup, and you tried to *pay* me."

He recoiled as though she'd slapped him. "That's
not what happened."

"Do you know what gaslighting is?" She scowled
at him.

"You were upset, and I was trying to help." He
squeezed the back of his neck, still embarrassed
at how that morning had gone. "You said—" He
couldn't remember what she'd said. Something about
having to get home right away because her brother
was reported as missing. He'd asked, "Do you need
money?"

She had looked at him like that. Like he was the
lowest form of life.

"I was trying to help. Money solves a lot of problems. I won't apologize for being wealthy," he stated.
It wasn't as if he hadn't been punished for it.

"Clearly it creates them, too," she said sweetly.
"Because I didn't want anything to do with you after
that. I still don't."

She walked into the bathroom and firmly closed
the door.

It was one of the best showers of her life, damn him.

Amelia was feeling grotty and sweaty from a very

tumultuous day, but was revitalized as the shower-head rained gently upon her face. The water was soothing and cleansing as it ran down her naked skin. Hotel-sized shampoo and other products were already in the bathroom, and they smelled amazing, producing bubbles that caressed her scalp and skin.

When she came out and moisturized with an equally delicious and fragrant lotion, she couldn't bear to put on her stained T-shirt. She gave in and tried on the blue-and-yellow polka-dot summer dress that had supposedly been purchased by Vienna, not Eden. Either way, it still had the tags and—

"Good grief," she muttered, eyes popping at the price.

It fit, though. Her bra straps showed beneath the tie straps and the bodice strained across her ample, padded breasts, but it would be easy to nurse in. The fall of soft cotton felt so lovely as it brushed her bare legs, she couldn't bear to take it off.

It also gave her a little more confidence when she went downstairs to meet the exquisitely put-together Carina and the even more chic Unity, Vienna's stylist.

Unity took Amelia's measurements and finger-combed her hair and held a few fabric swatches against her skin, then promised, "I'll pull some things together and come back in the morning." Unity departed, and Amelia went to the lounge.

Carina looked up from her tablet and smiled.

"Baby still sleeping?"

Amelia nodded and set the monitor on the end

table as she curled into the corner of the sofa across from Carina.

"Where's Hunter?" Was she doing this alone? Amelia looked around.

"He promised me coffee, but the service in this place is terrible. Oh, you didn't hear that." Carina bit her lips in pretended chagrin as Hunter appeared from the kitchen.

"Tip better," he suggested, setting a mug on the coffee table before seating himself next to Amelia.

Amelia looked at her nonexistent manicure and wished the sofa cushions would swallow her. The banter wasn't flirty. It was more like the comfortable trashing between longtime colleagues, but it still seemed to exclude her.

"Okay, so..." Carina tapped her screen. "Hunter brought me up to speed on the fact that you're considering marriage."

Amelia glared at him. "I didn't agree to that."

"I said we're talking about it," he said mildly. "We are."

"*You* are," she muttered.

"Obviously, we'll wait for the paternity results before making any announcements of that sort," Carina said in a soothing tone. "In the short term, we don't want anyone painting you as a home-wrecker. We'll circle back to talking about your family, but first I need all your best qualities, volunteer work, any friends in high places who might be willing to offer a quote? This is not a time to be modest. Gossip rags will approach your neighbors and anyone else they can find who might talk about you."

Amelia swallowed a thick lump of revulsion. Something touched her elbow and she snapped her head around as Hunter slid his fingertips down her bare arm, pulling goose bumps onto her skin before he captured her hand in his warm grip.

"It's okay. That's why we're doing this. To counter that sort of thing."

It was still awful, but she closed her hand around his. Clinging to his solidness made it a little easier to dredge up a few people who would say nice things about her. She made sure to mention that she tutored refugees online through a nonprofit organization, volunteering to help with their English as part of building her teaching résumé.

When Carina moved on to asking about past lovers, Amelia pulled her hand from Hunter's and tangled her fingers together in her lap.

"There's not much to tell. I dated in high school, but I had an overprotective brother so..." She shrugged wryly.

"I have one of those myself," Carina said with amused empathy.

Amelia experienced a stab of envy because Carina still had hers.

"What about university? Anyone serious there?" Carina asked.

"Just one. Gareth Bedford. He was a TA on another course and, um, cheated on me so I don't think he'll come out and say rotten things about me." She defensively slouched deeper into the corner of the sofa.

"You'd be surprised what people will say for their fifteen minutes of fame. When exactly did it end? Because speculation could emerge around Peyton's paternity. These sorts of things can linger. We want to be very clear there's no doubt."

Amelia snorted. "I'd like to see him try claiming he was her father when we never even had sex. If anything, he'll continue complaining about what a frigid prude I was."

"Oof. I'm sorry he was a jackass. I've met a few of those as well." She tapped her screen briefly. "Anyone else? Casual dates?"

"Like, coffee? What are they going to say about me? We traded notes from classes?" She shrugged. It had all been friendly, but benign.

"I'm not prying out of salacious interest, Amelia. This works best when we know who and what might come out to bite us."

"Us," Amelia repeated with a sniff of disdain.

"You," Carina acknowledged, taking on a kinder tone. "I'm only saying that this works best if you tell me about any intimate partners of any gender who might be brought to light and used against you. Forewarned is forearmed."

"I don't have any." She *really* wished she had stayed in bed this morning. To think, when Dad had come back and insisted on getting in the car, there had actually been a part of her that had latched on with enthusiasm to getting out of the house. She had thought the drive might be nice. Maybe they would pick up some sandwiches and eat them on the beach.

"Are we talking about the same thing?" Carina cocked her head, seeming perplexed. "Are you saying you've only slept with… Hunter?" Her voice rang with acute disbelief.

"I—" Amelia's heart lurched as she realized how much she had exposed of herself.

She could feel Hunter drilling holes into the side of her face with his gaze. Her cheeks started to sizzle, and her chest grew tight.

"Yes." Her voice cracked in the middle of the word.

"I see." To her credit, Carina didn't make a big deal of it, only said casually, "I'm not sure why you bothered with the paternity test, but it's good to know it will come back as expected. Let's talk about less favorable publicity. I haven't had time for a deep dive online, but I saw something about your brother walking away from his job site—"

"That is *not* what happened!" Amelia cried, lurching forward on the sofa cushion.

She was already wound tight enough to break in half. Now tears crashed into the backs of her eyes. She was suddenly short of breath, teetering on the verge of falling apart.

The cushion sank beside her as Hunter slid his hip right up against hers. The warmth of his body seemed to encompass her as his arm came around her hunched shoulders and he tipped her into his chest.

"This topic will be handled with the absolute, utmost care, Carina."

"Yes. Yes, it will," Carina assured him gravely. She nodded slowly and swallowed before she offered a tight smile. "I'll freshen my coffee and give you a minute, Amelia."

"I don't need a minute," she lied as she pressed her face into the hollow of Hunter's shoulder, but Carina was already gone and she was relieved. "I can talk about him," she insisted, even as she crushed the fabric of his shirt in her fist. "It's just been a really emotional day."

"It has." He shifted so she wasn't twisted quite so hard. He scooped her legs across his and dragged her into his lap. Then he just held her, light fingers drawing circles against the back of her shoulder. His chin rested on her hair.

She was shaking with the effort to fight grief and sorrow and despair. She slid her arm around his neck and clung to him as she clung to her composure. *Breathe*, she reminded herself. Breathe and let the wave of grief come up as high as it needed. It would recede in its own time; she just had to endure it while it was on her and in her.

After about four breaths, she realized he was inhaling and exhaling with her, guiding hers to become slow and steady. She clenched her eyes, and a tear squeaked onto her lashes. She sniffed.

"This is what I should have done that morning," he murmured, breath stirring the part in her hair. "I just wanted to help, Amelia. I swear that's the only reason I said what I did."

The money. If she hadn't been so distraught, she might have knocked her fist into his shoulder, but this felt so comforting, that old bruise faded into a vague memory.

"I don't want to cry," she said with a frustrated pang in her voice. "That has never helped. Not once."

"Stay right here as long as you need, then." He smoothed her hair and continued to rub her back.

She could have stayed like this forever, but hiccuped a few sobs before getting hold of herself and climbing out of his lap.

"It's okay. Tell her she can come back. I can do this." She just had to step into the hard shell she had worn every time she had picked up the phone or sat down to write yet another email that had wound up being ignored.

Hunter rose and invited Carina back into the living room.

"I'm really sorry, Amelia," Carina said as she retook her seat. "I thought— Well, it doesn't matter what I thought. You'll tell me the truth and we'll go from there."

Amelia started from the beginning. Jasper had been working in northern Alberta for a company that specializes in rare earth metal exploration. He was dispatched to Chile, where he was surveilling for a new project.

"The last time I spoke with him, he was excited because he'd realized they could sift through tailings from hundreds of dams. It's a greener endeavor than pit mining. The cost for the rights was dirt cheap, he said." She smiled faintly at that remembered pun. "The soil had already been displaced, and once the rare earth metals were extracted, it could be moved to better locations than where it had been left by the dam projects. He saw it as win all around. A couple of weeks went by and the next thing we heard, the company said he walked away with his interpreter. But why would he? He *wouldn't*. Something happened."

"No ransom demands?" Hunter asked.

"No. And no body." She clung to her elbows, still feeling so bewildered by this turn of events.

"Which company?" Hunter asked.

"REM-ex. Their HR manager told me—"

"I'll speak to their CEO." He pulled out his phone.

"Oh, good luck," Amelia huffed. She'd never gotten higher than a letter from the operations manager for South America advising her that they considered the matter closed.

She expected Hunter to leave a message with a recording or, at best, some low-level receptionist. He had it on speaker and set it on the coffee table.

"Hunter!" The male voice boomed into the living room. "I'm not taking work calls, but if you're on your honeymoon and want to meet up, we're anchored off Mykonos."

"I'm calling about Jasper Lindor, Orlin. You may have seen correspondence from his sister, Amelia?"

A pause, then, "Oh. Her. I'm familiar with the name, yes. Is she becoming a pain in your ass, too?"

"She's the mother of my child," Hunter said flatly. "Our marriage will bring her brother's disappearance back into the spotlight. You'll want better answers ready than the ones your people have been giving her."

There was dumbfounded silence, then a curse and a resigned, "I'll see what I can find out."

"Do," Hunter commanded. He ended the call without saying goodbye.

One call. Amelia had made thousands and had written a million emails and gotten absolutely nowhere. Hunter had made one call and got the man on vacation and got him to *promise* something.

Fresh tears welled in her eyes. Such a pressure grew in her chest, she couldn't speak. She didn't know if she was touched or outraged or hopeful or all of the above. Hopeful. Definitely hopeful. Her lips began to quiver. Her breath shook.

Hunter said to Carina, "Go check in with the team, see what you can get done with what you have so far."

"Sure thing." Carina flashed her a look as she quickly gathered her things and slipped away.

Amelia grabbed the tissue box like it was a lifeline and pulled some out. She jammed them against her running nose and brimming eyes.

"That's not a quid pro quo," Hunter said quietly. "I said we're marrying because it will light the largest fire under him."

"You'd think a man's life would do that, but..." She used the heels of her palms to hold the balled tissues against her wet eyes.

She didn't even care if Hunter had said it to black-mail her or make her feel beholden to him. She *was* beholden. She would marry him a dozen times over if it would give her the tiniest inkling of a clue as to what had happened to Jasper.

Apparently, he was right. Money could solve certain problems.

"Why—?" He cut himself off.

She blew her nose and dropped the tissues onto the table.

Hunter was looking toward the window, profile twisting with self-deprecation.

"What?" she prompted.

"Why didn't you tell me it was your first time?" His brows were bunched into a perplexed angle. When his gaze came back, it was filled with appre-hensive concern, "Did I hurt you?"

"Not too much."

He winced. "You should have said."

"I thought you'd think I was a weirdo, never hav-ing done it. I was twenty-three," she reminded him, and waved toward the elevator. "Did you see Carina's face? She thinks I'm a total weirdo."

"There's nothing weird about being a virgin. You haven't had sex and then you have. It's weirder that we make such a big deal of it. On the other hand..." He studied her. "If someone is holding off, there's usually a reason. Which makes me wonder, why that night? Why me?"

Her heart turned over in her chest. She buckled defensively over her folded arms, rocking slightly.

"This is a day when every single detail of my life has to be torn open and examined, isn't it? Do you want to hear about the day my period started and Jasper had to buy me supplies? Spoiler alert, he also bought a cake mix. It fell after he baked it and iced it too soon. It was literally the ugliest cake ever made, but I ate so much of it I still can't stand lemon-flavored desserts."

Tears leaked from the corners of her eyes down her temples. She clenched them shut.

"You don't have to talk about this, Amelia. I didn't mean to upset you."

"No, it's okay. I've never told anyone that, but it always makes me laugh when I think of it." She was smiling through her tears. "That's what he was trying to do, make me laugh. We'd lost Mom a few months before and he knew I really, really needed her that day."

"You miss him a lot."

"I really do." She picked up her head and cleared the thickness from her throat, swiping one more tissue across her face and resolving she was finished breaking down. "He also put the fear of Jasper into any boy who looked twice at me, mostly because he'd been through a pregnancy scare himself." She wrinkled her nose. "The girl actually went away with her aunt and only told him after she came back that it was all dealt with. She expected him to be relieved, but he was kind of messed up by it. Her body, her choice. He understood and supported that, but he was really adamant that if I was going to put myself in the position of having to make a choice like that, I should be serious about the guy. Not some random, you know?"

A harsh laugh cut from his throat.

"The irony, right?" She drew a pillow into her lap and hugged it. "When I started seeing Gareth, I explained that I wanted to go slow, that I needed to know we had a future before we had sex. He said he was fine with that, but whenever we fooled around, he was always pushing me to go all the way. He would pout when I made him stop, laying on a guilt trip. Some of that was my fault—"

"None of that was your fault," Hunter interjected firmly.

She waggled her head. "You're right. I know you're right, but I always think I should have seen him more clearly. There were other issues. He was controlling, but in a subtle way so I couldn't really argue with him. If I did, he would make me feel as though I was being petulant rather than standing up for myself. He wanted to tell me what to wear and who to talk to and what to say."

"Is that how you feel with me? Because I convinced you to stay here?" He drew his head back as though bracing for an unpleasant answer.

"No." She gave herself a moment to really consider the question, able to say truthfully, "I'm not thrilled that I feel stuck here, but you talked me into staying with facts, not manipulation. He always made it about him. He would say that if I genuinely loved him, I would want to make him happy. I knew I was putting too much pressure on myself to make my wedding night some big, romantic culmination, but I also didn't like feeling pressured by him. Even so, I was starting to think about doing it so he would shut up about it."

"That's a terrible reason to have sex."

"I know. Fortunately—I use that word loosely—a fellow student told me she was sleeping with him. She had just found out he and I were in a relationship and she was really sorry she had helped him be unfaithful to me, but she thought I would want to know. I did. I told him to kick rocks and he said it didn't count as cheating. He said we weren't really together since we hadn't consummated our relationship, but also, that's why he slept with her, because I wouldn't satisfy him."

"And you didn't order a hit? There's an app for that." Hunter curled his lip in disgust.

"Under self-help, I know. I made an account, but didn't go through with it."

"Ha," he barked. "At least you can laugh about it."

He eyed her with something like admiration, making her tingle.

"I did at first, yes." She brought her knees up and hugged them, resting her chin on top. "Then he spread rumors that I was frigid and uptight and whatever."

"What a piece of work. What's his name again? His Wi-Fi is going to become very spotty."

"Appreciated."

"Was it limited to campus, that gossip? Or online harassment, too?"

"Mostly on campus and it was embarrassing, but it wasn't untrue. Mostly. It meant that only two kinds of men approached me after that. The ones who thought I was a challenge—I'd been there, done that and no thank you to the headache. The other types were also waiting for their wedding night. They were nice, but I never met anyone who intrigued me enough to consider marrying him purely to find out what all the fuss was about."

Hunter had the one brow down again as he tried to make sense of all she had said and, perhaps, the things that she hadn't.

"Then I met you and you made me want to know what the fuss was about." She lifted a defensive shoulder. "You were open about it being only one night, which was refreshing honesty. I didn't know when I would meet someone else who made me feel like that, so I let it happen. And even though we ended on a sour note…"

His somber gaze reiterated that it had been a misunderstanding, not a payoff.

"I didn't regret it. I kind of thought, at least I had that one happy memory before we lost Jasper. Then I got *pregnant*, which made me feel like a world-class *idiot*."

"You're not an idiot. From what I've been told,

sex is the leading cause of pregnancy. We both took the risk, and here we are. You still could have told me it was your first time, though."

"Then I would have had to tell you all of that and we only had the one night, Hunter. I wanted to get to the good part."

"Oh." He smirked. "Same." He studied her, expression sobering. "Was it good? Worth the wait?"

She was dying, curled up as small as she could get, holding in not just self-consciousness, but that odd mix of excitement and sweetness and joy and unfettered lust that had exploded between them. It had been a good memory, one she had clung to through a lot of bad. One that made her daughter a precious gift.

"How would I know?" she asked wryly. "I had nothing to compare it to. You tell me." A hard, stinging blush heated her cheeks. Yes, she was fishing for a compliment. Some sign that it had meant something to him.

"I thought you were amazing," he said, voice pitched one note lower than usual. Shadows of conflict chased across his expression.

"Then why—" Her voice cracked, and she averted her face, not wanting him to see how badly she'd yearned for more from him. For some tiny sign that she had not been used and discarded.

He sighed. "I was in the middle of that mess with Irina. That's why Remy insisted I needed a weekend away. I didn't have the bandwidth for a relationship, especially one long distance. And..." He winced. "Vienna had already been nagging me to meet Eden."

"And you already knew she was more suited to you than a waitress who owed more than she owned. I get it." She nodded, devastated, but not surprised.

"Amelia."

"It's true. And you need to think about that before you spout off to Carina that we're getting married," she hurried to add. "It's one thing for me to privately feel that I'm not good enough for you. It is quite another for you to put me on the front page so everyone else can think it, too."

"Stop it," he said curtly.

"Don't pretend it's not true, Hunter! What would I bring to a marriage that even comes close to what Eden offered you?"

"Our daughter," he said sternly. "She outweighs all other considerations. She's the reason I'm not married to Eden right now."

"Listen to yourself!" She shot to her feet and took a few agitated steps away before she whirled on him. "You walked away from your wedding for *Peyton*. Not for me. I've said I'll work with you to have access. That doesn't mean we have to get married. What would I bring to our marriage besides potential for another child? Because this isn't Victorian England, Hunter. I need to be wanted for something more than my fertility. We don't love each other—which you've made clear isn't something you want—so what do I have that you want?"

He started to speak, clacked his teeth together,

then abruptly shot to his feet and walked away in the other direction. "Sex. All right?"

She choked out a laugh and waved a helpless hand. "You can get sex from anyone. If that's all you wanted, you should have married Eden. You could be having sex right now."

"I don't want sex with her. I want sex with *you*." He shoved his fingers through his hair, leaving it mussed. "I had to tell you not to text me. I was engaged. But if I hadn't been—"

Her ears strained to hear the rest. She actually took a few steps closer, trying to catch whatever he might say. Trying to see his expression behind the troubled hand that scrubbed across it.

"What?" she prompted.

"I haven't stopped thinking about you, Amelia." He dropped his arm to his side, the movement so heavy, it was as if he dropped a broadsword to the ground.

"Really?" She hugged herself. She wasn't even who she had always planned to become. That woman who was gainfully employed and living independently and confident in herself was far in the distance. She was still a stumbling, scuffed version of her. She was on her feet, but she was far behind where she wanted to be.

And that woman couldn't touch the Edens of the world—the ones with more than an education. A family name and a seat at the head of a corporate table and so many big-name friends, Amelia would have been starstruck today if she hadn't been the one in the spotlight.

"I want to ask how you could doubt it when that night was so fantastic, but…"

A humorless rasp sounded in his throat as he came toward her. His light touch grazed her elbows, thumbs sending goose bumps up her arms and down into her chest by barely caressing her biceps.

"I don't do that, you know. Pick up women. I wanted to believe I was blowing off steam, but even when it was happening, I knew it was more than that."

"What was it?"

"I don't know." His hands continued to caress her arms and shoulders, making her shake. "But I'd like to find out." His chin dipped so they were eye to eye. "Wouldn't you?"

In what she had thought were very twisted, messed-up fantasies, yes. She had longed to see him again and had felt wretched for it, as if she were that easily taken in again by a man who only wanted one thing.

That uncertainty still pulsed within her like an electric fence, keeping her holding a part of herself at a distance, but another part—the physical connection that had unraveled her that night—unfolded her arms and shifted her feet closer to his. She set light hands on his chest and felt herself nod jerkily. Her searching gaze slid from the stormy ocean of his irises and landed on his mouth.

Look at that beautiful mouth. That uncompromising bottom lip held a stern line as he brought it down on hers and *consumed* her.

A jolt, a savage blast of need, swirled around her, catching her up in a claw of acute passion. Maybe that was his arms closing around her, claiming her while he gently yet thoroughly ravished her mouth.

Had she expected some hesitant reunion? Not from Hunter. His confidence and his undisguised desire for her had drawn her last July. When he had looked at her, it hadn't been in a way that suggested she was a potential conquest. There'd been curiosity and heat and that wonderful control that said, *I want you, but I won't take you. You have to give yourself to me.*

Nothing and no one else made her feel like this. Hunter's embrace was unbreakable, but who would want to get away? She wanted to be closer and twined her arms around his neck, one hand splaying in his short hair so she could press him to kiss her harder. *Devour me. Make me yours. Forever. Now.*

A noise that didn't make sense caused Amelia to gasp and shove her hands against Hunter's shoulders, pressing him to let her go.

He had to consciously tell himself how to do that, because he'd fallen into a purely animalistic state that wanted to hold on to her for the duration of whatever was about to happen between them.

That noise was Peyton. Her cries were coming through the monitor.

As Amelia hurried away, Hunter bit back a groan that was both pain and relief. Pain because he was so aroused by their kiss, the denial of stopping physically hurt.

He was glad it hadn't gone further than that kiss, though. He had already revealed too much of himself. Too much hunger and—no. He refused to call it a need.

He couldn't believe he had confessed to all of that. It was lowering and left him feeling vulnerable that she knew how much he had craved another encounter with her. That night of theirs had kept talons in him for all these weeks and months since. He'd been thinking of her when he had finally given in to Vienna's prodding and asked Eden to dinner. His mind had been split between the past and the present when he proposed. From the moment his ring had gone onto Eden's finger, he had fought to forget a single night with a waitress he was convinced he would never see again.

Then she had reached out in November.

The temptation to say more than he had, to bring her closer rather than push her away, had been acute.

The very fact that he would think it, while engaged and moving down a far more sensible life path, had told him that Amelia was becoming the sort of obsession for him that Irina had been for his father. The same sort of weakness.

He had feared she would upend his life if he wasn't very, very careful, so he had told her he was committed elsewhere.

Don't text me again.

She hadn't.

That should have allowed him to put her firmly in the past, but it hadn't. The moment the first rows of grapes had appeared as he'd driven into the vineyard this morning, his libido had come alive with memories of sexual heat and shy touches and greedy lips and passionate cries. With the feel of her soft skin against his nude frame as he stretched awake.

That last, intensely satisfying tumble had been the hook. His orgasm-drugged mind had begun rearranging his world so he could bring her into it. He clearly remembered his sense of entitlement. *Why not?* He had mentally brushed aside duty and the importance of meetings with lawyers. He was a powerful man. The boss. He could do what he wanted. He could *have* what he wanted. He worked hard and *deserved* to have what he wanted. He wanted Amelia.

Into that slumberous arrogance, she'd picked up her phone and released a torn cry. Minutes later, she had dressed and left with that final, wounded look.

And she'd been a *virgin* that night?

He pinched the bridge of his nose, still trying to comprehend how he'd missed that salient detail. She'd been bashful, obviously feeling awkward, but the first time with any lover was always a little awkward. He hadn't thought anything of the nervous laughs and hesitant touches.

No, he remembered her passion. She might have been unschooled in the way she touched him, but her small gasps and moans and the way she had clung to him had told him she liked the way he touched her. That had turned him on like nothing else could. Her first climax had been against his hand, and her abandonment had almost taken him over the edge with her.

Maybe he should have realized her lack of experience when she had apologized for peaking so unexpectedly.

He recalled chuckling hoarsely, bemused, so horny he'd thought he would combust.

Had he rushed her at that point? He always wore a condom, always asked. She had said yes, she wanted him inside her, but he'd been aware of her tension as he pressed into her.

He'd thought maybe she wasn't as aroused as he was, having just climaxed, so he had paused and slid his touch between them, nearly losing it again when he found her dewy and taut. Her breaths had shortened as he teased her. She had clenched around his tip and her knee had come to his ribs and she had opened her mouth against his neck. Her moan of need had sent a vibration through his blood, straight to where he was penetrating her.

Slowly, slowly, he sank all the way in. It had been heaven and hell to hold himself still, hold back. He wanted to let loose, yet wanted it to last. Her arms had twined around his neck and she'd released a shaken sigh, pressing a tremulous smile to the corner of his mouth.

That was the moment he should have realized it

was her first time, but his mind had been fixated on the feel of her. His pulse had hammered in his ears, and his breath had been fire. They had started kissing and he began thrusting and she moved with him in perfect synchronicity. Her hands had been in his hair and across his shoulders and danced across his spine. Her legs had hugged him; her heels had been in his buttocks, encouraging him.

Pure torture and absolute paradise. His whole body had been a tense line of delicious self-denial, but he was determined to last for her. It had been hard not to give in to the pleasure crashing like waves over him, so hard the effort knotted his breath. The tingles of culmination had been gathering in his tailbone when her ragged breaths had become sobs of desperation.

Come, he had ordered roughly, as if he had the power to command it.

She had. Her inner muscles had clamped around him and released into the fluttering contractions that tripped his own powerful release. He'd nearly been ripped in half by the force of it. And loved it.

He ran his hand down his face, finding himself back in his Toronto penthouse with a rattled shake of his head. He was hard. Muscle memory, he thought ironically. He remembered every millisecond of their lovemaking, because he still replayed it in his highlight reel. She *was* his highlight reel.

She was his weakness, exactly as Irina had been for his father. Had he already forgotten that Amelia had ruined his *life* today?

On the baby monitor, he could hear her cooing to Peyton, laughing softly.

"How can you be hungry again? Okay, okay. Don't panic. I'm right here." Her voice faded as she moved away from the monitor, but he still heard her as she murmured, "So demanding. I wonder where you get that from?"

There was only amused indulgence in her voice, though. She loved their daughter without reserve. Did she really think that wasn't something he *required* in his marriage? Her capacity for loyalty toward family had tremendous value to him.

They had to marry. He still saw no other course of action that accomplished as many goals in one swoop, but he would have to be mindful of how easily she could influence him.

He would have to hold her at arm's length even when he was buried deep inside her.

Amelia had the fearful sense that if her daughter hadn't woken, she would be courting another pregnancy right now.

She gently smoothed her daughter's fine hair, thinking she would happily have a dozen more of his babies. This one was so lovably perfect, it was ridiculous.

Amelia was genuinely scared for Peyton, though. Hunter's world was as dangerous as it was luxurious. As she pulled her mind out of sexy kisses and back to everything Carina had said, she knew that marriage was the only way to spin their affair to keep Peyton from being crushed by the fallout.

Lust and a baby were not the strongest pillars on which to forge a marriage, though. The sort of marriage she had always seen for herself had been built on love and respect and liking. Friendship. Equality.

She didn't have any of those things from Hunter. Even his respect for her must be a thin version of it, given how she had forced this one-eighty on his life plan. Equality? Pah!

She drew the bodice of Vienna's dress back into place and shook out a fresh receiving blanket from the package of a dozen.

This was Peyton's life, she acknowledged as she gently swaddled her. Money wasn't everything, but it was something. Plus, as someone who had lost a parent, she knew the value in having a good relationship with the one who survived. She had to marry Hunter, for Peyton's sake. She knew that.

And she wanted to marry him. For her own sake. For the sex.

She clenched her eyes shut as she admitted it to herself. That kiss had been the same wild magic as their night last July. It was wonderfully exciting and dangerously disturbing. He made her feel weak. Helpless to herself and to him.

He made her want things he wasn't likely to give her, which made her deeply afraid their marriage wouldn't last.

Maybe she was best thinking of it as a continuation of their affair, one that would be a little messier to end than most.

Cradling her daughter against her shoulder, she found him downstairs taking the dishes from the living room to the kitchen.

"Everything all right?" he asked with a flicker of his gaze from her tense expression to the firm grip she had on their daughter.

"Sure. I'm dandy as hell. You?"

"Point taken." He set the dishes in the sink.

"Look. I know we have to get married," she began carefully.

He turned and leaned on the counter, arms folded across his wide chest. His expression was an absolute study in poker faces.

"Peyton needs your protection. I suppose I do, too." She chewed her lip, feeling hollow as she spoke of marriage so clinically, rather than with the excitement she had always anticipated she would feel. "It goes against everything I believe in to marry expecting to divorce, but that's what I think will happen."

"That's the spirit," he drawled. "Positive thinking is the secret to success."

"Do *you* think we have what it takes to go the distance?" she scoffed.

"I'm pretty stubborn when I set my mind to something."

"Like running a marathon even if it makes you vomit? That's the spirit," she mocked.

"We'll have a prenup," he said as if that was obvious. "If we divorce, it will be very civilized. I'll make sure of it."

That was the spirit she expected from him, she thought dourly.

"I don't care about your money. I need you to believe that. But I am concerned about what my life will look like."

"Finish school. Teach if you want to." He shrugged that off.

"I was worrying more about whether we would have more kids. I don't think that's a good idea. Not right away. I'm not ready to be pregnant again anyway. But I'll go on the pill or something. Obviously, condoms don't work for us."

"Oh. Yeah, of course." He pushed off the counter, all dynamic motion as he started back to the living room. "Whatever you're comfortable with."

CHAPTER SEVEN

THEY MARRIED THREE days later in the apartment.

Hunter offered to plan something bigger for another time, but Amelia brushed that off. She really did believe this union would be temporary. That's why she didn't take him up on the offer to fly her father in for the ceremony. Tobias had only just settled into the cottage at Lake of the Woods. He sounded content, so she would tell him after the fact.

Maybe she was also punishing Tobias for putting her in this position. He wanted Peyton's father to do the right thing? Fine. She acquiesced, but she wouldn't let her father see it and be all smug about it.

She wouldn't raise his expectations, then dash them in a year or two when she and Hunter admitted it wasn't working.

She asked Hunter to keep it to a bare minimum. Vienna was their witness, along with Carina. Apparently, Remy had read Hunter's invitation to be his best man again, but hadn't replied. Amelia could tell he was confused when his friend ghosted him, but the ceremony went on—not that it was very ceremonial.

She kept reminding herself that it was her choice to keep it so unsentimental and bureaucratic. Unity had shown her a dozen beautiful dresses of various lengths. Amelia had settled on a muted yellow pantsuit that Unity persuaded her to dress up with a satin camisole and a few sprigs of baby's breath in her hair.

Even that much froufrou nonsense bothered Amelia. She couldn't help recalling the vineyard and the string trio, the multitude of guests and linen-draped seats and the pavilion of fine china. That vision carved a hollow cavern into the pit of her stomach. Not because she wanted that. Not really. A thrown-together civil union would have been completely satisfying if she was marrying someone she loved, but she and Hunter didn't have that. *That* was the reason she felt cheated and unattached to anything that happened today.

Maybe if they had spent the last three days getting to know each other she might have felt differently, but they'd only come together for meals, and invariably someone had joined them. He had constantly been taking calls or meeting with strangers whom he would introduce very casually as, "Your driver while we're here," or "She's with the nanny agency. They're pulling some candidates together."

Amelia had been equally busy and inundated with decisions. Did she like this cut of neckline? Would she rather have her hair corrected to brunette or re-streaked to blond? Which brand of crib would she prefer for Peyton, and was there anything she needed from the house in Goderich?

She had left the penthouse only once for a visit to
the doctor. She took Peyton because she was due for
her first immunizations. That left the infant fussy
and running a low-grade fever. Amelia had opted for
an IUD, so she had cramps and was up with Peyton
half a dozen times in the night.

Hunter came in at four, concerned that Peyton
wasn't settling. He took her and walked her until
she cried herself out, allowing Amelia to finally get
some sleep.

They both had sunken eyes and a distinct lack of
spirit as they repeated their vows.

When the officiant pronounced them husband and
wife and urged, "You may kiss if you wish," Amelia
felt teary, and not in a good way. She was still angry
about all of this. She was sad that her life had become so much less than she had wanted for herself.
She felt cheated and raw and second-best.

Why had she agreed to this?

Hunter's strong hand cupped her cheek and his
mouth slanted across her own. It was a chaste kiss,
but the warmth of his palm brought heat to the surface of her skin. The brush of his lips made hers buzz
with subtle electricity that pulsed in signals down her
throat, through her heart and into her loins. Her lips
unconsciously caught at his, wanting him to linger.

The tip of his tongue brushed the seam of her
mouth, and she opened to welcome a deeper kiss. A
more thorough seal of their mouths and their union.
His touch on her arm firmed, and her hand fisted
into his jacket. She ran the other up and behind his

neck. His arm went behind her back and crushed her into the hard wall of his chest.

This, she thought distantly, as desire swept through her like fire through dry grass. This was why she had agreed. She wanted the sex, too. She wanted the run of his palm to her lower back and the shift of his body so she felt the brush of his growing erection against her stomach. She wanted to be wanted.

But even as she melted, Hunter abruptly lifted his head, setting Amelia back a step. He checked his mouth for smudged lipstick.

She pretended to care about her hair and used her raised elbow to hide whatever hurt might be showing in her expression. Then she sat to sign all the paperwork including a form to have Hunter added to Peyton's birth certificate.

She took Peyton from Vienna while they had their photo taken and accepted congratulations and sipped champagne when it was handed to her.

"It's a shame you didn't have time to get Peyton's passport sorted. A proper honeymoon would have been nice," Vienna said as they ate a light brunch. "The cabin is off-grid, though. At least no one will bother you there."

"I've never seen the Rockies. I'm looking forward to it," Amelia said politely. She had never seen Greece, either, but she was glad not to be subbing into the honeymoon Hunter had planned with Eden. "What time do we have to be at the airport?"

she asked Hunter, already dreading the long flight with Peyton.

"The plane is ready when we are," he said absently.

That wasn't an answer, but she bit back saying so.

A short while later, they said goodbye to their few guests. Amelia combed out her hair and changed into more comfortable travel clothes. When she came downstairs, Hunter was putting Peyton into her car seat.

"Ready?"

"No," she said with frustration. "I packed the diaper bag, but now I can't find it. Did you put it somewhere?"

"Everything has gone ahead. I've got the ticking time bomb— Yes, I know you hate being in this thing," he said patiently to Peyton as she squawked a complaint. "It's only a few minutes. I promise."

"I usually put my phone and wallet into it," Amelia grumbled, looking at both in her hands.

Unity had supplied her with a number of accessories, so she fetched a small purse with a long strap and only noticed the monogramed design after the fact. Goodness, the purse was worth ten times the amount of cash she was ever likely to carry in it.

She hurried to join Hunter on the elevator. "This doesn't feel right. The two times I went south for vacation, I was weighed down with bags and the stress of whether I had my passport and tickets. Do you use one of those first-class concierge services I've only heard about?"

The doors opened onto the roof, where a helicopter waited.

"Something like that," Hunter said drily.

The helicopter whisked them over the midday traffic to a private jet that was, indeed, waiting for them at the island airport.

Amelia had only seen planes like this in movies about drug lords and corrupt politicians. The interior was styled like a comfortable one-bedroom apartment with a king-size bed in a stateroom. The galley held a real stove, and the main salon had armchairs, a sofa, a big-screen television and a dining area toward the back. The decor was all polished wood and gleaming chrome.

The flight attendant brought champagne and gave Amelia the Wi-Fi code, instructing her to ring for anything she needed. After they got under way, she hung a swing seat for Peyton, but Peyton didn't care for it. Hunter wound up holding her. He urged Amelia to lie down in the stateroom, which she did, and she had the best nap of her life.

When they landed in Calgary, they hopped onto another smaller plane that took them to Banff. Only then did they travel by road—in a tricked-out four-wheel-drive SUV. A young man handed Hunter a key fob, and Hunter drove them through a winding route onto roads that weren't well-marked, but he seemed to know where he was going. Peyton must have been as enthralled with the scenery as Amelia, because she stayed quiet the whole way.

They arrived at massive iron gates that Hunter

opened with a touch of a button on his phone. He parked in front of a stone structure that was no modest cabin. It wasn't even a chalet. It was a castle with split levels and a round tower, angled roofs and massive windows that reflected the surrounding granite peaks.

"Why do you call this a cabin?" She had expected something far more rustic.

"It was a log home when my father bought it. He called this the cabin, and the lake house was the cottage, so we knew where we were going on vacation. Irina tore down the cabin and built this monstrosity about eight years ago. Way over budget, obviously. Vi and I still call it the cabin because we're very mature. But I told you it was a real house."

He hadn't told her it was a palace with *staff*. The caretakers were a young couple who volunteered on the ski patrol in the winter, "For the free ski pass," Kyra confided over her shoulder with a cheeky grin.

She showed Amelia into a room converted to a nursery, where Amelia put down the sleeping Peyton.

"I can listen for her if you and Mr. Waverly want to relax. There's a short walk down to a viewpoint. It has a picnic table. I could throw together a happy hour basket in five minutes if you like."

It hit her that she was Mrs. Waverly. That's why this young woman was treating her with deference even though Amelia was younger than she was and was technically still a jobless student.

"I'll, um, ask Hunter what he wants to do." She peeked into the hall.

Mr. Waverly had gone to change his shirt because Peyton spit up on him during the flight.

The double doors to the master suite were closed, and she almost knocked before entering, then slipped inside like a thief because she definitely did not belong here.

The room was huge with hardwood floors and a vaulted ceiling. There was a sitting area with a box window that thrust out, creating an impression of being suspended over the tree-filled valley where the turquoise line of a river snaked in the bottom of the crevice.

Hunter emerged from the walk-through closet that seemed to lead to what looked like a massive bathroom. He was shrugging on his shirt, fixing the collar. He froze when he saw her.

"Kyra said she would listen for Peyton if we want to go for a walk."

"We can do that." He finished straightening his collar, then lifted his head, eyelids growing heavy over his steady gaze. "If you want."

His voice dropped several octaves, hitting her like a stimulating vibration between her thighs.

She swallowed and looked to the window. Hugged herself. She was nervous about the sex, mostly because she was so eager. Embarrassingly eager. What if it was awful? What if they were married and stuck with each other and that night last year had been a combination of moonlight and ovulation?

"How long will she sleep?" he asked.

"An hour?" If they were lucky.

"Do you want to lock the door?" His voice was making her scalp tighten. All of her skin had grown sensitized. Nerve endings prickled beneath the surface. The air in her lungs thinned.

"I do, but—" She didn't move except to squinch up her eyes in a cringe of self-consciousness. "I don't know how it will be. My body is different. I'm worried it won't be good."

"I'm not." He spoke right in front of her.

She snapped her eyes open to see him reaching past her to click the lock.

"If something doesn't feel good, we'll stop and find something that does. For instance, that kiss the other day..." He cupped her face. "Felt very, very good."

"It did," she whispered, and watched his mouth come closer.

Then his lips were brushing hers, capturing. Her hands found his neck and the crisp line where the fade of his haircut met the hollow at the base of his skull. In seconds, they were back in that passionate kiss, and she was lost.

They both groaned, and he shifted his hands to the door behind her, flattening her there with the press of his body.

She gasped as she felt the shape of his erection press against her stomach.

"Yeah," he said against her ear, nuzzling her neck in a way that weakened her knees. "I think this new body of yours is really freaking hot."

She couldn't help but slide her hands beneath the

open edges of his shirt to explore the warm skin of his torso. She followed the ripples of his rib cage and found the lines of muscles in his lower back on either side of his spine. As they continued to kiss, she crept her touch back to the hard beads of his nipples.

He sucked in a harsh breath and lifted his head, pressing his hips into her, nostrils flaring as he looked down at her. He cupped her chin again.

"I'm trying to take this slow," he admonished through his teeth.

A thrill of power went through her, giving her the confidence to hold his gaze as she deliberately pushed back on him with the thrust of her hips, gently crushing her pelvic bone into his erection.

He made a supremely sexy sound, eyelids flinching before he swooped, gathering her up like she weighed nothing. Her stomach dipped and her head floated. She blinked and clung around his neck, trying to get her bearings, but she was disconcerted by his strength and the razor-sharp lines that had come into his intense expression.

"Did I hurt you?" she asked in surprise.

"In the best possible way, yes," he said grittily as he placed her on the bed. "Brace for payback."

Oh. She scooted to sit and drew her knees up. "I should, um, tell you that the doctor said I might need lubri—"

He withdrew a tube from the night table.

All her sexy feelings fell off a cliff. "Kept that handy for Eden, did you?"

"No." He scowled. "I did my research. You think

I wasn't interested in how soon a woman can have sex after a baby?" He caught her ankle and tugged.

She let him drag her down onto her back and remove one sock, but had to say, "I'm a little nervous. It's been a while for me, and you've been having sex with someone else—"

"I haven't." He threw her sock away and removed the other.

"But—" She was surprised. She let him pull her bottom all the way to the edge of the bed. "Sorry, I just assumed. You were engaged."

"She wanted to wait until we were married. Now quit talking about her."

She set her hands on the sides of his head, needing him to look her in the eye. "Is that true?"

"Yes. You're the last woman I slept with, okay?" There was such banked discomfort in his eyes as he revealed that, she couldn't doubt it.

"Okay," she said dumbly.

He threw off his shirt and dropped his trousers, his hurry implying it had been a while for him. She hid a smile at that thought and let him dispense with the fly on her wide-legged trousers. She lifted her hips so he could more easily peel them off her hips, then sat up to pull her shirt over her head.

He studied her as he absently dropped her clothes atop his own.

She bit her lip as he looked her over. Unity had bought her matching underwear with nursing bras that were a lot prettier than the boring white cotton ones she had gotten for herself. This one was gray satin with pink rickrack and a closure between her breasts that she found a lot more convenient than the strap snap of her old bras.

"I'm afraid to take this off," she said truthfully. "I don't want to spoil the mood if they decide to misbehave, but maybe a quick look?" She teasingly opened the cups to expose the heavy swells and the deep cleavage between.

"I think I have a kink for denial." He groaned as he sank to his knees between her feet. His gaze never left her chest. He grazed his tickling touch from her hips up her waist, making her nipples sting before he stole the edges of the cups from her fingers.

With great tenderness, he pressed a kiss to each inner swell, pooling his hot breath against her skin as he promised, "Another time."

He took great care securing the cups closed, then he made a noise of concern as he traced his fingertip up the flame-shaped mark on her abdomen. "Stretch marks?"

"Yes." She started to cover it with her hand, but he brushed her hand aside and gave her sternum a light nudge, encouraging her to lie back. He kissed and nuzzled along the marks, smoothing his lips across her abdomen and licking suggestively against the narrow waistband at her hip, then against her bikini line.

She was still a little tender from being waxed the other day, but when he opened his mouth and scraped his teeth over the silk covering her mound, such an

exquisite spear of sensation went through her she
nearly leaped straight up in the air.

"Hurt?" His eyes were laughing at her.

"No." But her legs had turned to jelly. Quivering
jelly as they tried to decide if they wanted to clamp
onto his torso or relax open for him.

"Do these have to stay on for some special reason?" He hooked his finger in the gray lace against
her hip.

Only because it was daylight, rather than the shad-
owy intimacy of midnight.

"You can take them off if you want to," she said,
voice husky with nerves.

"I do want to. Lift your hips."

He peeled the silk away, then stroked his hands up
and down her thighs. Her stomach jumped and quivered, and her muscles trembled. When his thumbs
came up to gently caress on either side of her sex,
her folds grew heavy and hot and sensitized. She
groaned and tried to twist.

"Do you want my mouth here? Because I'm dying
to taste you again." The pad of his thumb was tracing a line, barely, barely touching her. The most agitated, excited point on her body felt each pass of his
fingerprint like a lightning strike.

"I do," she admitted with a pang.

He drew her ankle onto his shoulder, kissing the
inside of her calf. "Do you think of that night?"

"Yes," she sobbed, throwing her arm over her
eyes.

"What do you do when you think of it?" His

mouth was traveling to the inside of her knee, arriving at the thin skin of her inner thigh. "Show me," he coaxed.

She was *dying*. Keeping her eyes hidden by one forearm, she slid her free hand down to relieve the ache he was stoking.

He groaned and his hair brushed her leg, then his mouth was against her, displacing and replacing her fingertip. His thumb circled her entrance, then eased in.

"Okay?"

"Yes," she groaned, digging her heel into his back and lifting her hips, losing herself to the sort of pleasure she hadn't known she could feel until she had met him. She had fooled around here and there. She wasn't a *strict* virgin, but that had been a biology class. This was…

She groaned out her enjoyment.

It was earthy. Erotic. Carnal in the way he turned her body into one receptive nerve ending. Filthy in the way he held her thighs open. Exquisitely pleasurable as climax swept up suddenly and crashed across her.

She realized belatedly that a cry had been torn from her throat. Had Kyra heard her? She might wake Peyton. Hunter didn't let that stop him. He aroused her anew, making it impossible for her to find breaths that didn't scrape and shake. Her breasts ached and her skin burned and a terrible, needy emptiness gripped her.

She licked lips that were dry from panting. "I want you inside me."

He turned his head and opened his mouth on her thigh, biting softly against the tendon there. Then he kissed her stomach and along the underside of her bra, her sternum and her collarbone and her chin.

"I don't think you're going to need this, but let's be sure." He reached for the lube and kicked away his boxers before smearing some on his erection with blatant confidence, fascinating her as she watched.

Then he lined himself up and played his glistening tip against her, pressing with incremental pressure at her entrance.

"It's okay," she gasped. There was a small pinch, no worse than their first time, which had had this same quality of hot friction and gratifying stretch.

As he filled her, the deep intimacy of the act made her eyes sting. This was the most vulnerable she'd ever felt, lying beneath him with his flesh inside her, but also the most alive and animalistic and, when he gently brushed her hair from the corner of her mouth, cherished.

"No condom," he said shakily. "I may not last long."

"I'll try to keep up."

"Do." He kissed her softly once, then more deeply, as if he couldn't get enough of her.

She shifted so he sank a fraction deeper, and he grunted with pleasure. Then he gathered her beneath him and watched her as he withdrew and returned.

"Okay?"

"Yes," she breathed, tracing his ear and arching sensuously. "It feels really good."

"It does." He combed a hand into her hair and kissed her deeply, moving with more purpose. "Really good."

They were made for this, she thought as she began to meet his thrusts, matching the pace he set. They were made for each other, because she was suddenly approaching another peak.

"Hunter—"

He paused.

"No, don't stop. Never stop," she gasped, so close. Almost there. "Don't stop, don't stop."

"Damn, woman." He kept thrusting, increasing his power.

Another profound orgasm rolled through her, nearly painful in the strength of her contractions, but so good she could only moan her pleasure.

"I thought I remembered this wrong." He made a sound between gratification and suffering as he gathered her and rolled her so she was above him.

For a few moments, she could only remain splayed atop him, nuzzling her nose into the crook of his neck while his hands stroked over her back and hips and backside.

He remained a pulsing presence inside her, so hard she couldn't help tightening around him. Soon he was subtly lifting his hips, and the pressure and slight friction brought her senses awake all over again.

She rose to sit straddled across him and roamed her hands over his chest, luxuriating in the right to do this.

His lips were pulled back against his teeth gritted in control. His hands firmed their grip on her hips as he urged her to ride him.

She did, watching through the screen of her lashes. The tendons in his neck stood out along with a vein on his arm. He might leave fingerprints on her buttocks, he was so fully in the grip of near orgasm.

"Let go," she urged, wanting to feel it, to watch him. She wanted to know she could make him unravel the way he kept devastating her.

"You first," he said in a voice so tight it was nearly menacing. He swept his thumb in and down, pressing between them so she couldn't escape the pressure as she rode him.

She didn't want to escape. Everything fell away except that pinpoint of exquisite sensation where he penetrated her. Her flesh tightened around him and shot shivering waves through the rest of her body.

"Hunter—" As her pleasure rose, she dug her nails into his chest and the marble-hard strength of his forearm. This shouldn't be happening again, but it was. She was nearly there. She lost her rhythm and ground herself against him, needing that. Him. Deep and hard within her as sparks danced behind her eyes and culmination reached up like a hand to grab her.

It was him. His hand caught behind her neck and

drew her down so they were kissing. Her cry was muffled by his own sharp groan as they shattered in unison.

CHAPTER EIGHT

"THAT WAS..." AMELIA'S voice faded as though she didn't have words.

Hunter didn't. His brain was nothing but fried wires. He was spent and gratified, still joined with his wife, who was sprawled upon him. *His wife.* Why did that satisfy him as deeply as the sex?

"A long time coming," she decided, then burst into giggles, stirring the hair on his chest and turning her smug laughter at her own pun into the hollow of his shoulder.

Tightness invaded his chest, but it wasn't a chuckle. It was a yank of discomfort at the truth in her remark.

"I'm sorry. Was that tasteless?" She abruptly lifted her head, sobering as she realized he wasn't as amused as she was.

"It was terrible. Worse than a dad joke. You're stepping on my territory." He smoothed her hair back from where the ends were tickling the edge of his jaw.

She searched his eyes, then gave him a smile as

pale as his own. When she shifted away, Hunter didn't try to stop her.

She slipped into the bathroom and he stayed where he was, throwing his arm over his head as he mentally probed at why he was so dismayed by something that was exactly the sort of dirty private joke a couple ought to share in the afterglow.

He didn't brag about conquests and had never been embarrassed by dry spells between lovers. On the contrary, it was a point of pride for him that he could go without sex, unlike his father.

But it felt too revealing that Amelia knew he hadn't slept with anyone since her, probably because self-discipline wasn't the reason he had put off having sex with Eden. Eden had broached the subject a couple of times, very cautiously. There had been a necessary timeline on their marriage, but they hadn't known each other well. He'd assured her there was no rush for intimacy.

The stark truth, however, was that he hadn't desired Eden the way he wanted Amelia. At that point, it had only been the memory of Amelia, interfering and preventing him from rousing to desire for Eden.

And once Amelia had been back in his life, it had been all he could do to wait the three days until they were married and she had some reliable birth control in place. How long had they been here? Not even an hour, and he'd been all over her. If he'd been able to manage it, he would have made her come three more times before he let himself finish.

He almost wished it hadn't been as good as he remembered. If he was disappointed right now, regretting this marriage, he wouldn't feel so raw. Instead, the sex had been *too* good. He was already impatient for her to emerge from the bathroom. Maybe they wouldn't have sex, but he wanted to touch her. Cover her. Kiss her.

He bit back a groan, flesh stirring with recovery. With want.

He didn't know her well enough for this to be an emotional connection. It was pure chemistry and hormones, which made it worse. His libido didn't care about little things like whether he could trust her.

If he wasn't very careful, he would become as besotted and stupidly indulgent as his father.

"I should unpack." Amelia reappeared wearing a fluffy white robe. She paused in the walk-through closet to stare at the suitcases that had been left there.

"Kyra will do it." Hunter made himself rise and find his briefs. They needed to get out of here or he'd have her on her back again before either of them knew it. "Let's walk. If Peyton is awake, we'll bring her with us."

Amelia wasn't sure what she had expected from her honeymoon—probably that she would get to know her husband better, but small things got in the way.

The most persistent small thing was their daughter. That didn't bother her. She enjoyed seeing Hunter bond with Peyton. He wore her in a sling while they took short hikes, never shied from changing her and even brought her to Amelia, saying, "That sounds like her hungry cry."

Other times the obstacles were more dismaying. They were out in public, where they could be over-heard. Or even in the house, Kyra and her husband were always nearby.

When she did get a minute to ask him something personal, Hunter always seemed to deflect. He was comfortable telling her facts—his mother had died from a blood infection when he was nine—but he didn't tell her how he felt about it.

"That must have been so hard. I'm really sorry." Amelia's heart ached for him.

"Vienna barely remembers her. That's why our family foundation raises money for treatments and cures for sepsis. The gala is next month, actually. I'll have my PA send you the details." He walked away to find his phone and issue that command.

He worked on and off, taking calls at odd mo-ments and disappearing to sit in on video meetings, which formed yet another thin wall between them.

Amelia couldn't help wondering if he would have done the same to Eden if he'd been sailing the Greek islands with her. Then she felt churlish because she was the one he had married.

She still didn't know what to think of his celibacy between July and their wedding night. It probably wasn't significant. Maybe Eden hadn't wanted to be intimate with someone who didn't love her.

Amelia wondered if there was something wrong with her that she did, because the other thing that came between their communicating with words was the constant sex.

She wouldn't call it lovemaking, because in a strange way, it felt almost like a sensual battle. They both triumphed, yet she always felt defeated. Sometimes it was a stolen quickie during naptime, sometimes it was a lazy, sleepy midnight coupling, and sometimes it was a lengthy contest where Hunter seemed determined to hold back through sheer strength of will while he found every single way he could wring moans and sobs and gasps from her.

She exulted in it, but also felt as though she was losing a piece of herself every single time.

She might have felt less dismantled if they had had a lazy day watching TV in bed, talking to no one but each other, but they went out every day. She didn't mind. It was beautiful. They walked to see waterfalls and ambled the shoreline of glacier-fed green lakes. They went up on the gondola one afternoon, and he took her out for dinner another evening. They lingered over dessert to listen to a folk musician. It was her first time leaving Peyton, but it all went fine.

They must have been recognized, though, because they visited an art gallery the next day and Amelia became aware of the stares they were garnering. Celebrities were common in Banff, but usually came in the winter months for ski vacations. That meant the paparazzi who made their living with candid photos had slim pickings this time of year. They were more than happy to settle for the Wave-Com cad and his strumpet wife.

That night they made the six o'clock news when it was reported that they were on honeymoon in Banff. The next day, they were photographed getting out of their SUV at the base of a hiking trail.

They got straight back in, not wanting to be stalked for the next two hours.

"It's okay," Amelia said as Hunter turned back toward home.

She was disappointed and feeling threatened and exposed, but she didn't think it warranted such a hard scowl as the one he was wearing. It made her feel the weight of being responsible for this scandal.

"I've been meaning to check in with Dad," she continued evenly. "Maybe I can catch him before he's out on the water again." He was fishing every day and loving it.

"Hopefully they're not at the gate when we get there," he said grimly.

Her phone pinged at that moment and so did Hunter's. Here in the mountains, they were in and out of service constantly. It wasn't unusual that both of their phones would buzz for attention simultaneously, but this seemed like more noise than usual.

Amelia glanced at her screen. Her messages were filtered, but she had set up an alert for Jasper's name. It was only a clickbait headline teasing his disappearance as a family trait. The article claimed Hunter was "hiding" his "runner-up wife" and her "money baby."

She told herself it was okay that she was getting raked over the coals so long as Jasper's situation was getting renewed visibility.

"What's wrong?" Hunter asked.

"Nothing. Just a nasty headline."

"Those aren't supposed to come to you."

"I can't keep from seeing all of them," she said, but he was already commanding his phone to "Call Carina."

"You got my message?" Carina asked as she answered. "I just confirmed it."

"Confirmed what?" Hunter snapped, glancing sharply at Amelia.

A pause, then in a confused voice, Carina said, "That Eden married Remy."

"Sylvain?" Hunter asked out of sheer astonishment.

Carina's swallow was audible. "Yes."

Hunter was quiet. Too quiet. Amelia couldn't tell if he was scorned or betrayed or embarrassed or furious or all of the above.

His only reaction was to say flatly when they got home, "The attention here is about to get worse. We'll go to Vancouver where security is easier to manage."

Within a few hours, they had landed in a drizzly Vancouver. After crawling across the bridge into West Vancouver, they arrived at a modern two-story home that, frankly, didn't look as welcoming or posh as the chalet. It was kind of boxy and had stone columns and a brick drive and a fancy front door, but Amelia was thinking that everyone who had ever complained about West Coast weather and traffic and the price of real estate was justified in their disparagement.

Then they walked inside, and she was confronted by one hundred and eighty degrees of windows. With suitable drama, Mother Nature turned off the rain. The clouds parted to allow rays of sunshine to crash onto platinum water. As she walked out to the terrace, a warm breeze that was sweet as pineapple kissed her cheek in greeting.

"Oh. Kay," she murmured. "I get it."

She walked back into the living room of white leather sofas. They were arranged to face a fireplace that looked through to the dining area furnished with space-age chairs and a glass table. The kitchen had a pass-through like a restaurant, but it was currently shuttered.

The house was built into the mountainside so there were several terraces at different levels, one overlooking the pool, another that offered a view of the inlet and the city skyline and a land mass in the misty distance.

"Is that Vancouver Island?" She squinted against the sheen on the waves.

"Yes. And always glance down there for orcas." He pointed.

"Get out of town!"

"True fact." He had pulled Peyton from her seat and was following her around, watching her reaction, but now said, "I have to make some calls. I'll show you where my office is so you can find me if you need me."

The housekeeper had whipped their luggage up the spiral staircase, not that there was much of it. Hunter had assured Amelia she should leave most of her clothes in Banff, claiming Unity had stocked *all* his homes with appropriate selections for the climate. *What did that even mean?*

He carried Peyton as they started down the spiral staircase. It also wound upward so the hollow space took up three floors and had spheres of modern art suspended in the column of empty air.

"Is Remy one of your calls?" she asked.

"If he wanted to talk to me, he would have called by now." Hunter spoke with so much frost, she sealed her lips.

They stepped off the stairs into a rec room tricked out like a pub with a full bar, a dance floor, a pool table and a dart board. There were comfortable pockets of seating and three televisions hung at convenient angles. Four sets of glass doors appeared to fold back upon themselves, opening the room to the patio and pool area. There was a hot tub out there as well. Hunter showed her a switch that ignited a semicircle of fire surrounding an outdoor eating area.

"Dramatic."

"It was built by a musician." He popped her eyes by naming one of Canada's most successful vocalists. "I bought it not long after I met you, actually."

"Did he let it go for a song? I couldn't resist." She bit her lip again.

"He did not." He didn't crack a smile.

She sighed inwardly. Did he blame her for his best

friend moving on his bride? Was he concerned that any hope he'd had of salvaging the business side of his marriage to Eden was now circling the drain?

"After the court case was over, I was ready for a change of scenery. Vi is in Calgary so I was planning to make that my home, but this came up. Then I spent three weeks out of four back east so I was planning to unload this and make Toronto my home again."

Because of Eden.

"You might prefer something closer to your father. We can talk about it as time goes on. That's salt water," Hunter said of the pool, continuing his tour. "Home theater." He moved to a windowless room at the back. It sat twelve in three rows of four recliners. "Gym." He opened and closed a door on a room full of equipment.

"Nanny suite." He flicked a wrist toward the back corner as he crossed behind the bar. "This is my office."

It took up the corner and was enormous. Two sets of French doors and a plethora of windows looked onto a garden that was in full bloom. The interior wall contained shelves filled with books and awards and art pieces. His desk was a shiny slab of ribbon-grained wood across two blocks of marble that were so big, she suspected the house had been built around them.

His phone rang so she said, "I'll leave you to it."

She took Peyton back upstairs, wondering if Hunter had bought this thinking he would raise his family here. The top floor held three bedrooms, all with walk-in closets and full bathrooms. One room was a nursery, and she thought the big one on the far end was the master since it had such a lovely view, but the closet only held a guest robe.

She went to the other end of the hall and *this* was the master. The walk-in closet here was a dressing room. It was lined with sliding doors and held a wall of shoe shelves, and there was a round upholstered bench in the middle. There was even a tailoring platform placed before a trifold mirror in the corner.

"I'm starting to think we're not in Goderich anymore," she whispered to Peyton.

The bathroom was as extravagant as everything else with French doors leading onto a private veranda and a massive shower that looked more like a sci-fi transportation device with nozzles and buttons and glass. In a bowed window, a jet tub invited her to relax and contemplate her life choices.

Amelia was questioning them. Big-time. Misgivings had been creeping in at every turn. While they'd been in Toronto, she'd been in shock, not fully appreciating Hunter's wealth until they had married and she had climbed aboard his private jet. *His*. Vienna had one, and there was a corporate one as well. In Banff, she had fallen into an illusion that she was visiting an all-inclusive upscale resort. It was a nice place to visit, but it wasn't her life. No one actually lived like this.

Except Hunter.

And her?

Things grew even more surreal as the day wore

on. People arrived. She met her personal assistant and her West Coast stylist. The housekeeper asked her questions about menus, and a prospective nanny arrived.

Amelia had chatted with the agency a few times through the week, shortlisting résumés, but it hadn't hit her that the decision to hire someone would rest with her—as it should, but it still freaked her out. She barely felt qualified to be a mother. Suddenly she found herself interviewing an accomplished woman her own age who had a degree in early childhood education, held a lifeguard certificate, and was fluent in English, French, Punjabi and Spanish, "Because my last family spent their winters in Mexico."

Matinder was not only more highly educated than Amelia, she was more prepared for Hunter's lifestyle.

Amelia introduced her to Peyton, who loved her, and Hunter, who asked questions around whether Matinder was prepared to travel internationally and whether she had pediatric first aid. She did. Of course she did. She had also worked briefly with a toddler who was hearing impaired. She knew basic ASL that she said would be useful for Peyton before she became verbal.

They arranged for her to start the following day.

"Because we have that party tomorrow night," Hunter added.

What party? Amelia recalled her PA asking if she wished to accept the invite while her stylist had promised to pull a few outfits together. She had told them to ask Hunter whether they would attend. Apparently, he had said yes.

Great, she thought with dread.

Hunter was still withdrawn at dinner, and Amelia thought a few times that she ought to try harder to discover how he was feeling about his best man marrying his bride. She kept thinking that if she couldn't bring sophistication and social cachet to this marriage, at least she could offer him emotional support.

He didn't seem to want that, so she began to quietly hyperventilate. Until now, all the pressure on her had been from the outside. Paparazzi followed them and people judged her, but she was mostly able to shrug it off because they didn't know her.

Tomorrow, however, she would have to step into a role that was completely foreign to her. When she organized a dinner or spoke at a fundraiser, she would make missteps and be critiqued on her decisions and actions.

No wonder he had wanted to marry someone like Eden. Amelia was going to embarrass him as badly as his stepmother had, and she wouldn't even do it on purpose.

When she got Peyton settled for the night, she found him waiting for her in their bedroom.

They barely spoke. She was so desperate for reassurance she went straight into his arms. Whatever emotions were churning within him translated into white-hot passion. His hard arms caught her close, and his hungry mouth ravished hers.

She sobbed with relief. Here she didn't have to

think about what a misfit she was in his life. Here they were equals.

At least, that's what she thought as he carried her to the bed. As they stripped and he came down to cover her, she pressed his shoulders, urging him to fall onto his back.

She was no shy virgin any longer. They had become familiar enough with each other's bodies that she didn't hesitate to pour herself over him, slithering her nudity against him and sweeping her hands over his shoulders and ribs and stomach. She was being more aggressive than she ever had been, caressing and kissing across his chest. His rib cage expanded beneath her lips as he drew a deep, shaken breath.

She loved it. She smiled and stroked her hands lower, caressed his powerful thighs and the flesh between, hearing him growl in pleasure. When she shifted lower to take him in her mouth, his hand on her shoulder tightened and he groaned like she was his salvation. Like he needed this. *Her.*

Excitement and sweet exaltation poured through her. She did everything she could to drive him wild, reveling in the intimacy. In the trust it implied. She was always the one to break first, but this time she would take him into that vulnerable place and know that she gave him *this.*

"Stop," he said in a jagged voice.

She lifted her head, feeling almost drugged, she was so lost to the act. "What's wrong?"

"What do you want?" His harsh question, delivered in that gravelly tone, didn't make sense.

"You." Wasn't that obvious?

"Take me, then." He dragged her up and atop him. "Do you need— No," he said with satisfaction as he caressed between her straddled thighs and found her slippery with desire. "You're more than ready, aren't you?"

So ready. She was shivering, holding still for his explorations because it felt so good. So necessary.

He held himself for her to impale upon and she groaned out as his thickness filled her.

This was better, she agreed hazily. She wanted them to be together when they finished. She began to move, losing herself in these rhythms they had taught each other. This was where they were not just equal, but the same. They wanted and sought as one. They reached and rose and lifted each other toward that pinnacle, arriving—

She shattered, dimly aware of his hips lifting hard beneath her. His hands gripped her waist, firm and unyielding. His grimace was one of ultimate control as he withheld his own release, leaving her to shudder and cry out and lose herself while he watched.

As she folded limply onto him, he rolled her beneath him and slowly began to pump, bringing her still-quivering senses sharply back to life. He knew exactly how to touch her, when to scrape his teeth on her neck and where to trail his fingertips on her breasts to make her nipples peak and sting. He knew how to lift her hips so the angle of his penetration hit a spot that had her arching with acute pleasure, a cry of anguished joy torn from her throat.

Then, only then, when he had her again on the brink of another explosive orgasm, did he allow himself to let go and take her over the edge with him.

That culmination, shared with him this time, was so powerful and glorious, it brought tears to her eyes.

But the sting lingered behind her eyelids when they were both weak and panting on the sheets. They weren't equals, she acknowledged, trying to swallow back the lump in her throat. She might be helpless to the chemistry that gripped them both, but he was impervious to it. Or at least, not as susceptible.

Maybe he had reasons for refusing to give up his control to her. Maybe he was determined to control *something*, given he was blindsided and helpless to do anything where his best friend and former bride were concerned.

Maybe she would know if he told her, but he only spooned her into his front and exhaled as his arm grew heavy across her waist.

Despite her physical satisfaction and growing lethargy, her lashes stayed wet and her mind continued to churn with angst. She was hurt and she was frustrated that he wouldn't share with her and she knew why it ate at her so relentlessly.

She was starting to fall for him.

Oh, who was she kidding? She had begun falling for him last year, when she had let a man she'd only just met take her virginity. She had been angry and scorned and deeply hurt when he didn't want to see her again. When he had told her he was marrying someone else, the rejection, the sense of a chance missed, had leveled her. She had blamed her weepiness on losing Jasper, but a large part of her depression at that time had been because there had been no more chance with the only man who interested her.

Then she had had his baby and had felt even more connected to him. That's why she had let him put her on this bullet train into his life. Here was her chance to see what they might have had.

But they had nothing.

That was the harsh reality she was beginning to face.

Perhaps not nothing, but a lot less than she had dreamed of.

As she realized what sorts of romantic ideals she had let form over that week of their honeymoon—that he might come to love her—she quietly cringed at how childish that vision had been.

This was her life. And she would have to live up to it.

CHAPTER NINE

HUNTER GOT UP with Peyton and was handing her over to the newly arrived nanny when Amelia came to find them. She was dressed, but her hair was in a messy clip and she was still befuddled with sleep.

"Why didn't you wake me? Isn't she hungry?"

"I gave her a bottle." Amelia had started pumping so he could feed her. "And we'll be out tonight, so I thought you should sleep in."

He tried reading her expression, but she became wrapped up in chatting with Matinder, so he left them to it.

The truth was, he had left her sleeping because she'd almost killed him last night. He'd awakened wanting her—that was constant—but he'd also been disturbed by how close he'd come to simply letting go last night.

He'd been tense after a long, restless day of ruminating over Remy and Eden. The oddest thing about that news was, once the initial shock had worn off, he discovered he didn't care.

He cared about them as people, especially Remy.

Hunter had met Remy in their first year of university. They had both been bored with the basic prerequisites they'd been forced to endure, going through the motions of earning paper credentials for work they already did. Unlike their classmates who were learning the theory of business, they had been deep in the practical trenches of their respective family corporations. Hunter had been leading Wave-Com's R&D team. "You're young," his father had told him. "Keep us ahead of everyone else." Remy had been running his family's airline with his grandfather. He'd been flying planes longer than he'd held a license to drive a car.

Aside from the tragic fact that Remy had lost both his parents while still in high school, Hunter had always envied him. Remy's family, spread among Paris, Montreal, Martinique and Haiti, was closely knit and very supportive of one another. Remy was good-looking, charming and smart. Everyone admired him for being a pilot and a talented vintner among his many other accomplishments.

"Chin up. No one likes the cable guy, but we all need him," Remy had noted once, proving himself sarcastically funny as well.

Remy was, simply, a good friend. As the court case had begun taking its toll on Hunter, when he'd still been reeling from his father's death, trying to keep the wheels from falling off the bus while fighting legal eagles and his dragon of a stepmother, Remy had insisted, "You need to unwind."

The weekend was supposed to be golf, a few

drinks and no phones. When the server at a micro-brewery had flirted with Remy, Hunter hadn't been the least surprised. He'd been taken aback that Remy suggested, "Ask your friend to join us."

Hunter had been lousy company and said so, but Remy had said, "For God's sake, man. Buy a pretty woman a drink and let her smile at you for an hour. That always cheers me up."

Now he came to think of it, that was the last time Hunter had spent any time with Remy. He had congratulated Hunter on the legal win. Vienna had hosted a small party to celebrate and Hunter had invited Eden since they had begun to date. Remy had arrived, but quickly mentioned another engagement.

When Hunter had called to ask him to be his best man, there had been a brief pause and a cryptic remark about a business rivalry with Eden's brother Micah. It had sounded like old news and something that happened across the pond.

"Who else would I ask? No one else would put up with me," Hunter had insisted.

"Then it would be my honor," Remy had assured him.

He had made an appearance at the engagement party, but hadn't lingered. He had attended Hunter's bachelor party, which had been another golf weekend, this time in British Columbia's wine country. Remy had jokingly had "the talk" with Hunter, asking, "Are you sure about this marriage?"

At least, Hunter had thought he was joking.

As far as he knew, Remy and Eden had only met

once before Hunter had reintroduced them, but now Hunter wondered. And even though he found the pair's rushed marriage strange, he discovered that he felt no envy for Remy. He should. His friend was marrying the woman Hunter had thought would be his ideal match. Hunter could no longer imagine being married to Eden, though. Not now that he was with Amelia.

He wasn't sure if he'd been misguided in his thinking when he had proposed to Eden, or was falling into the trap of self-indulgence with Amelia. Either way, it seemed he couldn't and shouldn't trust his own judgment.

That inner conflict had been eating at him when he met up with Amelia in their bedroom.

She had leaped on him in a way that had been gratifying. Too gratifying. His cynical brain had wondered if she was beginning to recognize her power over him and exercise it. Yet when he had asked her what she wanted, she had said, *You.*

Possibly the most ominous demand of all.

He mentally balked at letting down his guard. The barriers he had erected against her had to stay in place, for his own peace of mind, but he could tell she was nervous about tonight. He felt her agitation as she handed Peyton off to him, heading into a spare bedroom to have her hair and makeup done.

Hunter felt guilty for putting her through this. He had a learned aversion to parties, but a man in his position had no choice about attending at least some of them. Vi had always been a sport about going in his place when it made sense, but there was no avoiding this one.

This first appearance as a couple was inevitable, he reminded himself. He couldn't do anything about the clouds hanging over them, so he and Amelia would just have to power through.

He was nervous, he realized as he poured himself a second drink while waiting for her. This was the first time in a long time that he was escorting someone so important to him.

He shrugged against that word. *Important.* It wasn't wrong. Not only was Amelia the mother of his child, she was his wife. He cared about her, which was only right. A person ought to care about their spouse, but he didn't like how vulnerable his depth of caring made him feel. He didn't like how helpless he felt taking Amelia to a party where she would be measured against Eden.

He wasn't concerned for his own sake. He didn't care what people thought of him. If there had been a bright side to Irina's constant scenes, it had been to forever inoculate him against embarrassment. His depth of concern for public opinion only went as far as caring how it affected the company. It was his job to watch for bad publicity and fix it.

Amelia, however, was not so impervious to censure. He'd seen it when she had caught glimpses of online troll dung. She wanted to reflect well on him and Hunter wanted to say a weary, *It doesn't matter.* People would talk behind their hands regardless.

He heard her on the stairs and turned, catching

a glimpse of her legs. Never mind stopping traffic. Those stems stopped his heart, playing peekaboo through the uprights as she picked her way down in a pair of gold sandals with rhinestone buckles against her ankle and a lethal heel.

The rest of her appeared in a short, sleeveless dress in a nude color with gold beading in geometric patterns. The weight of the beads caused the fabric to rest against her curves in the most arresting way.

Her hair had been cut before the wedding, removing the blond, leaving a rich brunette curtain that landed on her shoulders and flipped up with a vintage flair. Her makeup was only slightly heavier than what she applied herself, but it managed to make her eyes look bigger and darker, her lips plumper, and her skin radiant.

"Unity picked it out," she said self-consciously as she came to a halt halfway toward him. "I thought it disguised the fact that I was still carrying some baby weight, but it's too short, isn't it? Now that I've put on heels?"

"Define 'too short.' Because I think you look hot as hell."

"I'm supposed to look like your *wife*." She plucked at the hem.

"My wife can't be hot? Change if you're uncomfortable, but I think that's perfectly on brand. For you, actually, not just for my wife. You were wearing something much shorter when we met, and it suited the hell out of you, same as this."

"Big surprise that all you can remember about me is my legs." She flicked her hair behind her shoulder.

"Excuse me, but your legs are not the only thing I remember. They're not even the first thing that drew my attention." They were the second. "I heard you laugh and it was so engaging, I turned my head to see what the joke was." Then he had caught an eyeful of her smiling profile, her pretty legs and ample breasts and straw-colored hair. He had immediately tried to pretend to himself and Remy that he wasn't mesmerized.

She made a noise of uncertainty, looking down. "You really think this is okay? Because I feel like people are going to talk about me behind my back."

"They absolutely will. Let's give them something to talk about." He waved her to come closer and reached for the box he'd left on the end table.

"Oh," she murmured as she realized it was a jewelry box.

"This is where I went today." He opened it to show her the necklace with rose-gold links in a basket weave pattern. Seven pink and white stones were interspersed between them across the front half.

"It's beautiful, but— Wait," she said, balking when he drew a circle in the air, indicating she should turn and lift her hair. "Those aren't real, are they?"

"You think I bought you glass and plastic? They're diamonds and pink sapphires, yes. Why? Don't you like them?"

Her eyes grew wide enough to swallow her face.

"I'm already nervous, Hunter. I can't walk around wearing something so expensive. What if I lose it?"

"It's insured. And I don't know any jewelry designers who go to the trouble of making art hoping it will sit in a safe. Show it off. Turn around."

She did, and he set the chain against her throat, closing it behind her neck, then setting a kiss there, wanting to linger and breathe in her fragrance of almonds and whipped cream.

"Is it a special designer? Why are people going to talk about it? What should I say if they ask?"

"That it's your push present."

"What? Hunter!" She whirled to face him. "Push presents are a fad created by advertisers to sell stuff to gullible dads."

"It worked. But I am very grateful for our daughter, you know." He traced a line along the inside of the necklace so it was a perfect arc beneath her collarbone.

She shivered, and he would bet this necklace that her nipples had just peaked behind her nursing pads. It was a heady enough thought to have him considering blowing off the party and heading back upstairs.

"I'm grateful for her, too," Amelia said with a hint of impatience. "Does that mean I owe you a trinket for your manly effort in punching through a condom?"

"Ha!" The remark caught him so off guard, he couldn't help laughing. Damn, but she knew how to lift him out of whatever ruminations he was trying to wallow in. "I appreciate the thought, but no."

"Well, I didn't need anything, either, but thank you." She set her hand on his lapel and lifted her mouth to invite his kiss. Her pleased smile at making him laugh was so cute, he took a mental picture.

For one second, he thought, *I don't need anything else, either. Only you.*

"There's more," he said, eschewing the kiss and clearing his throat. He stepped back to take her hand while he fished in his pocket. Then he slid the diamond ring onto her finger.

"No. Hunter. We talked about this. Oh, gosh," she said helplessly. Covetously.

When they had prepared for their wedding, she had said she only wanted a plain wedding band because she didn't want to accidentally scratch Peyton. They hadn't been engaged, she said. It would be silly to wear a ring to signify the handful of hours before they married. They had settled on a platinum band with three baguette diamonds, and there hadn't been a matching ring, anyway.

Hunter had spotted this one today, though, while he'd been picking out the necklace. Seven baguette diamonds stood at different heights like a miniature city skyline. When it sat nestled against her wedding band, the effect was not unlike the hazy silver shape of Toronto against the glittering water as they'd stood on the shoreline last year.

That sounded far too sentimental and romantic to admit, though.

"People will expect you to wear one, so put it on when we go out. I'll give you the combination to the safe in the bedroom. You can store it there when you take it off."

"Okay. Thank you." She made a micro adjustment to the ring, lashes lowered, voice subdued. When she lifted her face, her smile wasn't as warm or bright as it had been, making his stomach pitch.

"Careful of my makeup," she said as he lowered his head to kiss her. "Let's not give them *that* to talk about."

Amelia was so nervous her hand was clammy in Hunter's as he drew her into the party.

As if the pressure couldn't get any worse, their host turned out to be a television personality. His wife held this solstice party every summer to celebrate the longest day of the year. The point was to arrive before sunset, so it was eight o'clock. The rain had ceased and the cloudy horizon was turning pink and pale gold.

Conversation lulled as they entered. Several pairs of curious eyes turned on them.

Amelia felt a pinch on her ring finger and realized she had tightened her grip on Hunter's hand, causing her new ring to dig into her flesh. What a scaredy-cat.

She didn't want to think about that ring, either. For a few seconds, she had been charmed and delighted. If the necklace affirmed his joy at having a daughter, the ring must be a symbol of his gladness at marrying her, right?

Then Hunter had reduced its significance to carrying an umbrella in case it rained. *People will expect it.*

"Hunter!" Their hostess approached with a beaming smile. "We're so glad you both could make it."

"So are we." He introduced Amelia, and they began making the rounds.

Her on-and-off career in the service industry came to her rescue. The ability to gauge when and how much small talk to make was a surefire way to improve tips.

Each time she met someone new, she asked a variation of, "Where's home?" or "Where do you plan to travel next?"

She liked to make the other person feel superior, too. She said, "I'm dying to get to know the Okanagan labels. Which wineries do you recommend?" and, "That's my father's team. He would disown me if I didn't root for them, but he's not here so I'll secretly agree with you. They're playing terribly this year."

Hunter stood by, interjecting with his own droll remarks, making her feel safe and funny and pretty. She began to relax and enjoy herself.

That's why she was so aghast when a viper struck.

A woman who had had one too many leaned in to ask, "What do you think of this sudden marriage between Eden Bellamy and Remy Sylvain? Sounds like Hunter wasn't the only one stepping out. What can you tell me about it?"

"Nothing," Amelia blurted, falling back on something her mother used to say. "There's no such thing as harmless gossip. It always stabs someone." She wanted to cringe as soon as the pompous words came out of her mouth. Who did she think she was?

Clinging to her last shred of dignity, she said, "Would you excuse me? I should check with our nanny."

She hurried away without even looking at Hunter, far too mortified that she had done the one thing she had sworn she wouldn't. She had embarrassed him.

CHAPTER TEN

AMELIA WAS SITTING in a quiet window seat on a landing, trying to compose a text to Carina to explain her behavior, when she realized with a lurch of guilt that Hunter was coming up the stairs toward her.

"Is Peyton all right?" he asked. "You've been gone a while."

"Totally fine. Fast asleep. Matinder showed her to me over video chat." Which had made Amelia feel like a helicopter mom, among other things. She gathered her courage and just blurted it. "I'm really sorry I embarrassed you. I shouldn't have said that to that woman. She took me by surprise, but that's no excuse. I'll keep my cool next time, I promise."

"Is that what you're doing up here? Self-flagellating? That woman embarrassed herself. For God's sake, Amelia. There is a vast difference between standing up for yourself and tearing someone else down." He leaned his shoulder against the wall. "I'm the furthest thing from humiliated. I'm glad to know you can hold your own when someone crosses a line."

"Really?" Her vision blurred she was so relieved.

"Yes, really. Come here." He drew her to her feet and into a warm hug. "And thank you for refusing to gossip about them."

"It was the truth," she said with a scrape in her throat. "I barely know them. Their marriage doesn't affect me, so I have nothing to say."

"Except?" he prompted, as if he heard the word silently tacked to the end.

"Unless…" she corrected into his tie, then lifted her gaze to his, making herself put this into words. "Unless their marriage makes you regret ours?"

"No," he said firmly, frowning with confusion. "Why would it? My only regret about our relationship is that it caused me to hurt Eden. I feel like I led her on." His mouth curled with self-disgust. "That wasn't fair. If she has since found consolation with Remy…" He shrugged. "More power to them."

She studied his expression, searching for shadows, but he looked and sounded as though he was being completely frank. She offered a crooked smile.

"Thank you. I was feeling really sick about that." She nodded toward the party. "I felt like I'd been rude to a customer and was about to be fired."

He snorted. "First of all, if one of us tries to fire the other, a lot of lawyers will get involved, so let's save it for a truly heinous offense, like leaving the cap off the toothpaste. Also, that woman isn't your customer. She is definitely not always right."

"True, but…" She slid a finger along his tie. "I

feel like I have to impress people and I'm not... impressive."

"I was thinking the complete opposite." He rubbed her back. "You're better at putting people at ease than I am. They enjoy chatting with you."

"Oh, please," she scoffed.

"Hey. *I* wanted to spend more time with you. That's the reason you wound up in my room last year. If I'd found you boring or unpleasant, I wouldn't have invited you to join me there, killer legs notwithstanding. Be yourself, Amelia. Be polite until someone breaks that social contract, then do what you did and stop giving them your time."

She was so touched, she hugged him and the words almost came out of her. *I love you.*

For an extra second, she held on to him, eyes closed as she absorbed the rainbow of refracted emotions that shot into every corner of her being. Sparkling gold and passionate pink, earnest orange, possessive green and a true blue edged with dark indigo shadows of knowledge that he didn't love her back.

He kissed her temple.

"And listen. I don't care if people think I sneaked away with my wife to neck in a stairwell, but if that's what you want to do, we should go home and do it properly."

"We'll stay for another twenty minutes. Let's not be obvious."

"Deal."

* * *

Over the next weeks, things settled into a comfortable routine.

Hunter went into his downtown office a few times a week, but worked from home on the other days. He took her to Calgary for a two-night trip, mostly so she could visit with Vienna while he was at work. Auntie Vi suitably spoiled her niece with dozens of outfits and toys, admitting while Amelia opened them that she and Neal had been trying to conceive for two years.

"I'm so sorry." Amelia let the panda-patterned romper drop into her lap. "It must have hurt so much when I came along with my unplanned, first-try surprise."

"Not at all. I'm happy for my brother. And I'm only twenty-five," Vienna dismissed with an overly cheerful smile. "We have time to explore options if it doesn't work out naturally."

"I'm sure it will." Amelia left it at that, but it was a good reminder that even someone like Vienna, who seemed to have everything she could ever want, still struggled with things that felt basic to existence.

Amelia mentioned it to Hunter when they were back in Vancouver a few nights later, enjoying a rare evening at home. "Did you know Vienna and Neal are trying for a baby?"

"I did." He hesitated, as though not wanting to say too much. "She's wanted to start their family for some time."

Does Neal? She closed her mouth against saying

it, but while Vienna had taken every opportunity to cuddle Peyton, Neal had barely looked at his niece. Not everyone liked other people's children, Amelia understood that, but for a married man starting a family, he talked an awful lot like a bachelor on his way to a sporting match with his toxic friends.

"How long have they been married?" she asked curiously.

"Four years." He mentally calculated. "Coming up to five."

"Gosh, she married young."

"Unlike us," he mocked drily, then sobered. "I tried to keep her from rushing into it, but Vi had her reasons."

"Such as? You don't have to tell me." She immediately corrected herself. "It's just that she said something at, um, the wedding. I keep thinking about it."

"What was that?"

"That it's not as easy to call off a wedding as it sounds. I feel like only someone who has actually contemplated doing it would say that."

"Little did she know it's easy as hell. Just walk away," he said with a darkly ironic curl to his mouth, then he grimaced. "I wish she had called it off. She had a more complex relationship with our father than I did. He assumed I would take over and I was interested in the business. No matter what else went on, what disagreements we had, we always had that common ground to come back to. Vi didn't have the same connection with him, but she wanted to feel like she was contributing to our collective benefit.

Her marriage to Neal looked very good on paper. His family made their fortune in video rentals, eventually expanding into entertainment tech and home computers. It was a good fit to merge that under our umbrella, and Neal is a savvy salesman. I can't deny he closes deals."

"But?" she prompted.

"But I can't stand the man. He cheated on her at his bachelor party. I told her to call it off. Dad told her to get over it and finish what she started. She listened to him." He stabbed a breaded oyster and ate it.

"He didn't have much sympathy because his wife cheated on him?" she guessed.

"Or didn't care that she did? I don't know why he thought Vi shouldn't be upset, but I had a chat with Neal. He understands that any future infidelity won't be tolerated by *me*, though he still finds ways to be a jerk to her. I support her having a family if that's what she wants, but I also want to tell her to cut her losses. It's a tough line to walk."

His protective older brother act always made her wistful for her own.

Which reminded her in a roundabout way of something else they needed to discuss.

"Vienna told me your birthday is coming up—"

"I don't celebrate it," Hunter cut in flatly.

"She told me that, too." She smiled faintly at how firm he sounded. "She didn't say why."

"We're cleaning out the entire family closet tonight?" He sighed and picked up his wine, taking a healthy gulp. "When I was turning eleven, Irina arranged my birthday party. It was the first time she had done something nice for me. My whole class was invited along with their parents. I realize now, as an adult, it was an excuse for her to stage a raging party for day drinkers. At the time, it felt like I was cementing myself as Most Popular Boy heading into middle school."

Another big gulp, then he set his glass aside.

"You also have to realize that I wasn't as inured to her behavior as I am today. This was the first time I'd really seen that side of her. She got worse over the years. Much worse, but this was my first exposure to her being a sloppy drunk and making off-color jokes about how long I spent in the shower."

"Oh, no. Hunter, I'm so sorry."

"I'm not even there yet," he assured her, holding up a hand. "Dad thought it was hilarious. All the other parents were laughing. I felt like the biggest tool alive when I was forced into the decorated chair, the center of attention as I opened all my gifts. I didn't want anything except for the day to be over. I didn't open her gift. I pretended I didn't see it and, once everyone went back to eating their cake and ice cream, I took it into the house. I was going to throw it away in the laundry room, but there they were."

Amelia sank back in her chair, asking a dread-filled, "Who?"

"Irina and one of the dads. I didn't even have a full grasp of what sex was. I sure as hell didn't know you could do it by dropping your pants around your ankles and bending a woman over the washing machine."

"*No.* That's *wrong.* A child isn't equipped to process that!"

"Tell me about it. I felt like I was in the wrong for seeing them. I didn't know whether I should tell my dad. I was sick about it."

"Was there anyone you could talk to? Your grandparents?"

"I would have taken it to my grave," he said grimly. "But about a week later, Dad got on me about how I was treating her. I couldn't even look at her. She told him I was sulking because I'd caught her in the laundry room. She told him flat out in very blunt terms what she'd been doing and with whom. Like it was a joke that I'd seen it and was upset about it."

"What did your father do?" There was an ache behind her breastbone as she watched old emotions paint across his face—anger and humiliation, impotence and disillusion.

"He blustered about how I should have knocked."

"No," she breathed.

"I heard them arguing in the bedroom later. It didn't last long, and she was still there the next morning. She was always still there." He took another gulp of wine. "And somehow that other man's wife found out. I didn't tell anyone, but the kid blamed me for his parents' divorce. It was my party where he cheated. That stuck to me for years."

"I'm so *sorry.*"

"Not your apology to make. And like I say, her antics grew worse. I learned not to give her opportunities. No more birthday parties."

"And your father stayed married to her." She couldn't believe it.

"He did." He nodded.

Amelia felt so sad for both him and Vienna, having to grow up and grow a thick skin when they should have been able to make their own mistakes and have their father be there for them the way hers had for her.

"Thank you for telling me. I just thought it was contradictory. Vienna said you don't celebrate, but when she told me the date, I thought it must have been the reason for your golf weekend last year."

"No." He shook his head. "That was a mental health break that happened to fall on my birthday. But that's *our* anniversary," he realized. "We can celebrate that. We'll go for dinner. Or would you rather make a weekend of it? Visit the Okanagan?"

"Actually…" She folded her arms in front of the plate she had yet to finish. "It's also the anniversary of Jasper going missing. I'd rather spend it with Dad, if you don't mind. He's heading back to Goderich this week."

Hunter swore and sat back. "Of course. I didn't even think. I need to spend a few weeks in Toronto anyway. We'll visit him from there. Let me know if he has any trouble with paparazzi once he's home. The security system was installed, but that will only protect his privacy while he's inside the house."

"Thanks. I will." He was doing so much for her father. For all of them. She hated to ask for more, but, "Since we're on the topic… Have you heard anything from your friend? About Jasper?" There had been a few brief news pieces that had coincided with the coverage of their marriage.

Amelia Lindor, sister of Jasper Lindor, who went missing in South America last year and is presumed deceased...

She was glad his disappearance was being noted again, but it didn't seem to be pushing anyone to investigate further.

"To be clear, I golfed with Orlin at a charity tournament once. That's as well as I know him. He sent their internal investigation to my PA, but it doesn't say anything more than what you've already told me. They do mention a life insurance policy," he said in a very neutral tone.

"And that I've pushed them to pay it out? I know how that looks." She picked up her fork, but had lost her appetite.

She could feel the weight of Hunter's suspicion in his gaze.

"Think about it," she rushed on with subdued fury. "They say we have to wait seven years for that money because there's no proof he's dead, yet they want us to believe there's no reason to investigate further. They know I'll use that money to hire someone to go there and look for him so they refuse to pay it."

He blinked, but not before she saw the shadows of pity behind his eyes.

"I know I'm grasping at straws," she muttered, dropping her fork with a clank. "But you don't know what it's like to come up against someone like you! All the power is weighted on your side. All the money and information and…" She picked up her napkin and pressed it to her stinging eyes, lungs seized by injustice.

"You want someone to blame. I understand that, but I have nothing to do with this, Amelia."

"I know that." Her mouth still quivered with futile anger. With frustrated loss. Her heart was cracked in two and there was a part of her that felt as though marrying him was consorting with the enemy. "But if Jasper suddenly reappeared, he would find me living like this. He would think I had completely forgotten about him. What if he's hurt, Hunter? What if he can't get home and I'm not even trying to help him?"

She was going to fall apart.

"I have to check on Peyton." She rose abruptly and threw her napkin over her half-eaten meal.

"Amelia." She had the sense his hand came out behind her, but she hurried away.

Hunter's first reaction when he had read that Amelia was pressing for the insurance pay out had been a cynical one. Money fueled all things, all people. That's what he'd been taught, and it was borne out by his lived reality nearly every day.

Nearly.

Amelia wasn't motivated by financial gain. He had known that when she'd thrown his money back in his face as she walked out of his room last year. Amelia ran on love, especially where her brother was concerned.

Hunter didn't take it personally that she had flared up at him. He understood. Grief had its own cycles, and he still became moody in April, which was the time of year when his mother had passed.

Also, he might not be at fault for Jasper's disappearance, but he felt some guilt as he brooded on it. He *was* the type of Goliath she and her father were up against. More pertinently, he could have done more for her that morning when the disappearance happened. He hadn't wanted to involve himself in someone else's drama, having enough in his own life.

Her anguish ate at him. He asked her to send him her file of correspondence and spent several days going through it.

It was a relentless and heart-wrenching effort on her part, shaking every tree she could find without success. His own grim conclusion was that Jasper was gone. Her brother had been sent to Chile to survey specific terrain. Against instructions, he had gone a different direction. This was the source of their "walked away from the job site" claim. A month or so into his disappearance, there had been a landslide. His interpreter had been among those found in the rubble.

Amelia's argument was that Jasper understood the dangers of the mountains. He had worked in avalanche control for several winters. He would recognize dangerous conditions.

Hunter was skeptical that anyone could have such a heightened sixth sense, but he couldn't shake the contradiction she had pointed out. Why wouldn't REM-ex pay out the insurance if they were so confident her brother was dead?

He made discreet arrangements for boots on the ground in Chile. At least his own conscience would be satisfied that he had done all he could for her.

He didn't tell her, though. He would wait for the report. The last thing he wanted was to tease her and Tobias with false hope.

Amelia was subdued when they arrived at her childhood home two weeks later. It was a small bungalow in a modest neighborhood, well maintained with a tidy yard. Peyton's bedroom was filled with secondhand furniture, but it had clearly been assembled with care.

The somber reason for their visit was lightened by the baby. Peyton was becoming a real character with an infectious giggle and an expressive face. She always wiggled and crowed with excitement when one of her parents reached to pick her up and, cutest of all, she remembered Tobias. He sat down in his chair and held out his arms. As Amelia bent to place her in his lap, Peyton gave Tobias a brief look of confused anxiety, almost seeming about to cry, but the second he took her, she folded right into his chest.

"It's that scratchy beard," Amelia teased, pinching her father's whiskers. "I would know a hug from you blindfolded. Like a baby duck imprinting on its mother's feathers."

"This little duckling is sure getting strong," Tobias said with gruff affection. "I can barely hold on to her."

It was a touching moment that put smiles on all their faces, but later, when Hunter came back from changing Peyton, he found Tobias trying to comfort Amelia through a very weak moment.

She was sobbing uncontrollably, and Tobias was saying gruffly, "No, chicken. He wouldn't want you breaking your heart like this. Shush now."

Something cracked in Hunter's chest, ringing a hard enough ache through him that he had to take Peyton back into her bedroom and breathe through it.

As he rocked his child, he had to wonder how he would cope in Tobias's shoes. Not well, that was for damned sure. This little sprite was so much a part of him, he couldn't imagine his life without her. As for her mother...

He couldn't stand that Amelia was hurting. He did have all the money and power and influence, as she had accused him, yet he couldn't fix what was wrong for her. He had a half dozen homes, all big enough to fit this one inside it, and she didn't care. She only wanted what he couldn't give her. It was humbling.

She slipped in to join him, wiping a balled-up tissue under her eyes as she asked in a tear-hoarsened voice, "Is everything okay? You didn't come back."

"It looked like you and your dad needed a minute." He lifted his arm with invitation.

She pressed herself to his side, slipping one arm

behind his back. The other encircled their baby, who sleepily left her head on his shoulder.

For a few breaths, they stood quiet, both watching Peyton chew her fist.

"Sometimes I wonder if Jasper's spirit made her happen," Amelia confided softly, brushing a tender hand over Peyton's fine hair. "Maybe he knew she would give me and Dad a reason to keep going after we learned he was gone."

Hunter hugged her closer and pressed his lips to her forehead.

Then he had to admit, "I don't actually find the idea of your brother being in the room with us last summer very comforting."

She hugged herself into him and shook with laughter, muffling it against his chest.

He smiled past the ache in his tight throat, pleased he could give her that at least.

CHAPTER ELEVEN

BEFORE THEY LEFT, Amelia tried to convince her father to move to Vancouver. He wanted to stay in his home and continue to see his friends every day, but he agreed to visit soon.

Wistful, Amelia hugged him goodbye and left for Toronto with Hunter.

"You'll have time to pop out and see him again before we go back to Vancouver," Hunter reminded in a consoling tone. "Would you feel better if we moved here so you would be closer to him?"

"I'm not sure. I like Vancouver." She had started to make a network of friends there through a baby group. "But I worry about Dad feeling lonely, even though I think he found it stressful for us to live with him. He felt a lot of responsibility to provide for Peyton and keep up with her, but he's not as spry as he was when Jasper and I were her age."

"That's why he found the man who is responsible for her," Hunter noted. "I'm glad he did." He looked down at Peyton with such tenderness, Amelia's heart fluttered. "We don't really have to decide until she starts school, but give it some thought."

"Are you being considerate? Or do you really not care where we live?" It seemed laughable to her that he would leave such a huge decision up to her.

"Both. I can tell that your father's house is what home means to you—retreat, security. Memories, I suppose." He shrugged. "You want to be deliberate about where you make one with me and Peyton so you can foster those same things, but I don't have that same desire for attachment to the place where I sleep. Comfort and convenience are my priorities."

Because he didn't have any *good* memories of home?

She felt such pity for the child he'd been, unable to *be* a child who felt safe and happy in the place where he slept.

"What?" His gaze sharpened and his expression stiffened at whatever he read in her eyes.

"Nothing." She looked away, hiding the melancholy she felt on his behalf. "I'm just wondering if I'm comfort or convenience?"

He snorted and picked up her hand to kiss her knuckle. "You're the luxury touch that makes one place more appealing than another."

"Ooh. Nice recovery," she teased.

They arrived at the penthouse then and kicked off a busy schedule of Hunter disappearing for meetings and other work commitments while Amelia planned dinner parties and attended engagements with him most nights.

When she had a moment, she conducted a discreet search online to see if Remy and Eden were in town. They seemed to be in France, and Amelia wasn't sure if she was relieved by that or not. Hunter was still being circumspect about that strange twist, but when Amelia looked at photos of Eden, the other woman looked so beautiful and put together, Amelia felt inadequate all over again.

She was getting better at this role of society wife, though. She enjoyed hosting a dinner for some of Hunter's executives and meeting their spouses. Thanks to her father, she was enough of a basketball fan that, when she and Hunter were invited to watch a game from the private box of a famous rap star, she had a great time.

Still pondering whether to make Toronto their home, she arranged a brunch for a handful of her old friends. She had lost touch with many of them in the last couple of years. They had finished school and started their careers while she had stayed home with her new baby and concentrated on finding Jasper.

It was fun to catch up, but she felt...different. Not better or worse than any of them. She was picking up the bill with a credit card her husband had given her and she didn't have a job of her own, so their opinion of her could have gone either way, but she knew she wasn't the person they had known a year ago. Jasper had changed her. Peyton had. *Hunter* had.

She had been raised to be independent, yet she relied on him. He could have made her feel small or resentful of that, especially after the way she had ruined his life plan with Eden, but he empowered her with decisions like where they would live. He made an effort to do his share with Peyton, saying, "I'll bathe her," leaving her to finish her book.

And sometimes, he did ridiculous things to spoil her, like when he took her to a charity gala aboard a restored tall ship in the harbor.

Amelia was feeling proud of her marriage and confident in her new self. She wore a sassy gold evening gown with a cutout at her cleavage. The skirt turned to fringe past her knees, showcasing her sling-back brass-colored sandals. Her hair was in a loose topknot with a few tendrils around her face, something that drew Hunter's gaze to her diamond stud earrings right before he made an obscene bid for a pair of chandelier earrings set with a half dozen pear-shaped yellow sapphires.

"You just called them gorgeous," he said when she nearly choked on her champagne. "They would suit that gown better than the ones you're wearing, and it's a good cause. You want to support them, don't you?"

"As if I could say no when you put it like that." The charity was a children's hospital foundation. It was a very good cause.

"Okay, then. Buck up and accept them."

What an absurd man. She had to laugh as she leaned into him, giddy. It wasn't the earrings. It was the way he looked at her with amused affection while making his illogical argument, as though he knew how to tickle her funny bone and was smug that he'd found it.

In that moment, she loved him so much, the declaration lifted like helium in her chest, expanding in her throat. The words formed against her tingling lips.

"I lo—"

"Amelia?" a male voice interrupted.

She drew back and turned with a polite smile that faltered as her new life collided with an old one she had escaped via a painful wormhole.

"Gareth. It's nice to see you." Not. She could have lived her whole life without ever seeing this particular man's smarmy face again. He was handsome, no doubt about it. A regular Viking god with blond hair and golden stubble and a shiny tailored suit.

Most of the men had removed their jackets because the heat of the day lingered, even here on the water after the sun had gone down. Gareth still wore his double-breasted jacket buttoned closed, and Amelia knew why. His shoulders were padded and the cut gave him the wedge shape that he coveted, but didn't naturally possess. Gareth was all about how things looked, his female companions being of particular importance to his controlling eye.

"This is my husband, Hunter Waverly," Amelia said. "Gareth was a TA at my university."

"Professor now," Gareth said as he shook Hunter's hand. "Philosophy and English Lit."

"Ah. Good evening," Hunter said in a circumspect tone that Amelia had learned to read. His instincts were far better than hers. He already saw Gareth for what he was. She had been far too easily impressed by Gareth's superficial gleam.

She smiled at the woman by Gareth's side, expecting him to introduce her.

Gareth continued holding Hunter's cool stare. "It sounds like a quick trip to the altar. I've seen the news." He shifted his razor-sharp gaze to Amelia. "And you have a baby? How did that happen?" He made it sound like friendly teasing, but Amelia was still sensitive to that honed edge in his "jokes." How had Hunter pried open her legs, Gareth was asking.

She stifled a flinch of old scorn.

At the same time, she saw the young woman's smile fading into insecurity at being overlooked. Amelia saw *herself.* The other woman was twenty if she was a day, exactly the age Amelia had been when Gareth had impressed her with parties like this. He didn't have money, but he leaned on calculated social connections for invitations to things like this. He loved to seem wealthier and more popular than he really was. All of it was designed to elevate his ego and make others feel worthless.

"I'm Amelia." She thrust out her hand at the woman. "How are you enjoying the evening?"

"Chelsea. Hi." She grew flustered now that she'd been noticed.

"We're having a great time," Gareth said, throwing a possessive arm around Chelsea and speaking for her.

"You're one of his students?" Hunter asked as though he already knew she must be.

"No!" Chelsea's eyes widened in horror.

"It's summer break," Gareth reminded him smoothly. "We met at the end of last semester. She's not going back so..."

So it was okay for him to prey on her, even though Amelia estimated their age difference to be at least twelve years. She had every confidence that Chelsea's decision to put off going back to school had been Gareth's decision more than her own.

"You're enjoying the auction," Gareth noted, narrowing his eyes at the bid sheet for the earrings. "Driving up the bids." *As usual*, his tone said as he slid another look at Amelia.

What are you holding out for?

A future. Do you want to marry me or not?

Today, the idea of being married to Gareth made her sick. What a narrow escape she'd had! Poor Chelsea was still stuck in his quagmire, though.

"What were you studying?" Amelia asked her.

"Oh, um, marketing?" Chelsea flickered a glance at Gareth, who had no doubt been critical enough that she now questioned any passion or talent she'd had for the field.

"That's good luck." Amelia looped her hand around her husband's arm. "Hunter was saying yesterday that there would be positions opening up at the Toronto office once the interns left in September. You should apply."

"You should." Hunter didn't bat an eye at Amelia's

fabrication. He reached into his pocket for a business card. She had never felt so connected to him on a purely psychic level. "Call that number and leave your name with my assistant."

"That's not necessary." Gareth tried to take the card.

Hunter held on to it and said very frostily, "I'm not talking to you." *Ever*, was the implied period on that sentence.

"Thank you." Chelsea swallowed and read the card.

Amelia instinctually knew Chelsea was memorizing the number because she fully expected Gareth to take it from her, costing her an opportunity.

"DM me on social media if you lose that," Amelia said with a warm smile. "It will take me a few days to get back to you because I don't check it myself. Some people are trolls." She dropped her smile and looked to Gareth. "Would you excuse us? I should check with our nanny." It had become her code to Hunter that she wanted out of a given conversation.

"Let's find a quiet corner. Good night." He nodded at Chelsea and turned away from Gareth without another look.

Hunter was jealous. It was a new color on him and one he didn't care for. At all. Especially because it wasn't even warranted. It had been plain as day to him that Amelia couldn't stand her ex. Also, he knew for a fact that her physical relationship with that egomaniac hadn't been as intimate as the one he currently enjoyed with her.

Even so, she had given that other man enough of her heart to leave it bruised. He recalled her talking about how Gareth had controlled and manipulated her. She gave that other man time he hadn't valued. Time he hadn't deserved.

Hunter wanted that time back. For her and for himself.

He was affronted, too. Disgusted that a professor had moved on her. He remembered her vaguely mentioning he was a TA during that first meeting with Carina, but it had slipped his mind with so many other things going on. And maybe Gareth had been a teaching assistant at the time and not on her course, but it still seemed wrong. Hunter was already planning to make a call to the chancellor. His family name was on the business program, and he signed off on generous donations every year. He sure as hell wouldn't be associated with a school that allowed its faculty to con students into dropping out so they could screw them.

"I feel like I should apologize," Amelia said as she returned to the bedroom from feeding Peyton. Their daughter had seemed to sense their return, waking as Amelia had been changing out of her gown. She had hurried down the hall in her robe, hair still up and jewelry still on.

"I feel like *I* should apologize," Hunter muttered. "He's the kind of man who makes all of us look like scumbags."

"He makes me appreciate that you're *not* like him. You must be wondering how I could have had anything to do with him, though." She sat down on the edge of the bed and removed her earrings, dropping them into the dish on the bedside table.

"I know how," he said with a snort. "You were young and inexperienced and *kind*. You give people the benefit of the doubt, always wanting to see the best in them. It annoys the hell out of me that he took advantage of that."

"That's a nice thing to say. I think." Her lips wobbled in a rueful smile. She looked at her fingers as she worked her engagement ring off. "I was gullible, but I became cynical after I stopped seeing him. I didn't believe any man was who he pretended to be."

"Is that what you thought when we met? That I was pretending to be someone else?"

"Kind of. I knew who you were so I knew you were rich, but I didn't think you were rich like this." She looked to the ceiling. "When I got into your room, I thought you had only booked it to impress whatever woman you brought back to it."

"I wasn't planning to bring anyone back to it," he said, insulted.

"I know that now." She lifted a shoulder. "And at least you were up-front about your lack of intentions."

"That wasn't my best moment," he noted with self-disgust. "I shouldn't have invited you to my room at all. We weren't as equal as I thought at the time." Virgin. He still couldn't fully grasp it. "I can't help feeling I took advantage of you."

"No, that's the thing. It was the first time a man had made a move on me who wasn't trying to make me feel guilty if I refused. I genuinely knew it was my choice whether to go with you or not. Weirdly, I felt like if I said no, I would be saying no to myself. It's hard to explain. I just knew I would regret it more if I didn't go with you than if I did. I had never felt like that with anyone else."

"Then you did regret it because you thought I was trying to pay you for it."

"I did hate you a little bit for that," she admitted, pulling her hair free. "It confirmed my worst suspicions of men, but thinking the worst becomes a habit that paves a straight road to despair and depression. With Jasper missing, I needed hope. I made myself look for the good in life. REM-ex gave us the runaround, but so many of our neighbors and friends were supportive and generous. Then Peyton became such a blessing. She's a little joy machine, so how could I stay a pessimist?"

"True." He chuckled, but drily. Amelia might have been disillusioned by Gareth, but Hunter hadn't exactly redeemed his sex. "I was in a terrible headspace last year. Still grieving Dad and even though I wasn't the least bit surprised by Irina going after the company, I couldn't believe it went as far as it did, legally. There was even a part of me that thought, hell, take it. The idea of not being responsible for Wave-Com sounded like heaven."

"You did mention that you were grumpy. Maybe Remy said that." She fiddled with the tail on her robe's belt. "I just remember Cheryl and Remy doing all the talking while I sat there wondering if you were interested in me at all."

"That's funny." He released a gust of laughter as it suddenly came back to him. "I remember waiting for *you* to show some sign of interest. I don't know if you know this, but I'm rich and reasonably good-looking. I make great babies that come with all the latest features."

She snorted. "That *is* news to me."

"I'm used to women making it clear when they're interested, but you played it pretty damned cool."

"Oh? Tell me more about the women who come on to you. Maybe text it from one of the other bedrooms," she suggested with a flutter of her lashes and a sugary smile.

He ignored that. "Your friend was throwing herself at Remy, but you were quieter. When you did speak, you were funny, but you didn't say much about yourself. I wanted to know more. That's why I suggested we walk down to the water after they left. All you said was that it was a pretty night."

"Oh, gosh. Big surprise you weren't interested in more than a night with that brilliant conversation going on," she muttered with self-deprecation.

"No. I remember thinking how refreshing it was." He had the sense of a time slip. For a moment, he was there on the shore with her, coated in quiet blue light. "Everyone wants something from me." Attention or money or favors. Conversation. A diaper change, he thought ironically. "Even Remy, with the best of intentions, insisted I give myself a break to golf with him. You said it was a pretty night. It was a simple observation that didn't require me to agree or decide or do anything except stand in it with you. That made you precious."

He had held her hand, and there had been music in the distance and sweetness on the breeze. It had been the first time since childhood that he'd felt so unencumbered. So at ease.

Then they had kissed, and his brain had wanted to know her better in the more biblical sense.

The way she was looking at him made his heart seesaw in his chest. Having her in his life was like having potent wine and spring sunshine and hope on tap at all times.

Skepticism had been his stalwart friend for so long, he didn't know how to replace it with her, but he wanted to. She was softness and peace, and she brought light into the gloomy caverns inside him. She was a gift, and he didn't know how to make her understand how precious she was except to show her.

Hunter pressed his mouth to hers in the most tender way, achingly gentle so Amelia felt like the most treasured thing in existence. He cradled the back of her head and worshipped her with his touch, shaping the hills and dips of her figure, setting small fires across her skin that licked their way into her erogenous zones.

They made love often, but this was the first time it *felt* like love. As she basked in the sweet way he kissed across her cheek to her ear, as he blew softly against her neck and made her hair stand on end, she closed her eyes and pressed more deeply into him.

It meant so much to her that he'd wanted to know more about her. *Her.* Their baby might have brought them back together, but their connection had been there from the beginning, the tiny, barely visible strands as strong as they were fragile. Precious.

When his lips came back to hers, she poured her soul into their kiss. Her passion. Her love. It felt so good to let it release without fear, holding nothing back.

His chest expanded as though he felt it. He squashed her breasts as he held her closer and deepened their kiss. She swore she could feel his heart pounding behind his rib cage, matching the urgency that was taking hold in her quickening blood.

This moment felt urgent yet not. She needed more of him. All of him. But they had their whole lives to discover every last thing about each other. They were still learning how to share their bodies and their hearts, and this was one of those times where they had moved into a new level of intimacy. Of caring and adoration.

Maybe he felt the same contradictory urges. He yanked at his shirt, then jerked open her belt, dragging her bared chest into contact with his.

She shivered and went on tiptoe, offering a deeper kiss, accepting his tongue and rubbing her hips against the steely shape behind his fly. She wanted him to know what he did to her. Only him. It had to be him.

"I want to be inside you," he rasped as he skated his damp lips down her throat. "I could lose myself in you. I really could."

"Yes." That's what she wanted, for all of him to overwhelm her. Fill her up and dissolve any barriers between them. "I'm yours." *Be mine.*

They skimmed away their clothes, and he pressed her to the mattress beneath his naked heat. She opened her legs in welcome, but he only guided himself against her wet folds, teasing and readying both of them before he slowly entered her.

They both released shaken sighs as he sank deep and held himself there.

Now the urgency subsided. They were where they needed to be. She looked at him through vision that was hazed by love and lust. His green-gray eyes were equally glazed by passion, and his kiss was soft again. Tasting of benediction.

Now they existed in a place of pleasure and profound connection. Love. She loved him so much. And he was hers. Forever. She stroked her hands possessively across his shoulders and traced her fingers down his spine, smiling when she caused him to draw a breath of delight. She rolled her thumb across his nipple and slid her hand to where they were joined, making him growl as she played her hand there, pleasuring them both.

"You'll make me lose it before you're even close," he warned, dragging her hands up beside her head.

She would love to. Just once. "Would that be so bad?"

A shadow moved behind his glittering gaze, just enough to tell her that it would be. For him. She didn't understand that reservation in him. Weren't they surrendering to each other right now? Didn't he trust her as completely as she trusted him?

She would have cupped his jaw, but he kissed her and began to move with more purpose. She groaned, luxuriating in the powerful way he thrust and withdrew, driving both of them toward the pinnacle.

This was all she needed in life, this man moving within her, making her feel exalted as he sent shuddering reverberations of pure joy through her nerves and muscles and blood.

"Hunter," she gasped, arching in the throes.

"Let go, angel. Come so I can."

As if she could hold back. She was there, clinging to him as her vision turned to gold and her skin caught fire and her inner being melded with his.

"I love you," she cried as the world fell away and orgasm crashed onto her like a hundred-foot wave. "I love you. I love you."

His answer was a tortured noise of agony and a crushing embrace as he pinned his hips to hers and his whole body shuddered in his own defeat.

CHAPTER TWELVE

HUNTER'S HEART COULDN'T seem to settle back into his chest. As the thunder of climax subsided, his heartbeat shifted into an uneven, more suffocating rhythm.

Amelia came back from the bathroom and slipped on her nightgown before she slid into bed.

Most nights he was sorry for that thin barrier between them. She wore it so she could rise and go to Peyton if needed. Tonight, it was a necessary layer in the wall he was trying to shore up between them as she snuggled close into his side, resting her bent knee across his thigh. She settled her arm across his tense abdomen. Her head found the hollow of his shoulder and fine hairs caught against the stubble coming in on his jaw, exactly as it always did.

He smoothed it with his free hand, letting his other arm curl around her.

But he wouldn't fall into a dead sleep the way he usually did. An underlying tension ate at his core.

I love you.

She wasn't as boneless as she usually was, either.

She didn't sigh and drift off. He felt the blink of her lashes tickling his skin.

I love you.

From the very beginning, he had sensed she could wield untold power over him if he wasn't careful. The very fact that they'd wound up in bed that first night when he'd had no intention of taking her to his room had warned him that he had a weakness where she was concerned. That's why he continued to fight the depth of passion she was able to wring out of him. That's why he held on to his control every single time they came together physically. He never let go until it was on his terms, not hers.

His fear had always been that if she gained the upper hand sexually, she would exact something from him—concessions and indulgence like his father had offered to Irina time and again. Hunter didn't want to be humiliated by his wife. He didn't want to be controlled by her.

Slowly, he had begun to believe Amelia would never ask anything from him that he wasn't prepared to give, but now he realized she would. Had. She wanted his heart.

Once he gave that up, there would be nothing left of himself. She would own him completely.

"Should we talk about it?" she asked with soft apprehension.

He could have pretended he was asleep, but that would have been the coward's way out. And it only would have prolonged a conversation that would have to happen regardless.

Trouble was, he didn't know what to say.

There was a long stretch of silence where neither of them moved. Then she swallowed and moved away to her side of the bed.

"It's fine if you don't want to say it back." Her voice broke in the middle of that statement, proving it wasn't fine at all.

He silently swore and set his arm across his eyes, wishing it hadn't come to this because he was going to hurt her. There was no way he would lie to her, though.

"You have to remember where I come from, Amelia. What we have here, in this bed, is incredible. But it scares the hell out of me. I've seen what sexual infatuation does to a man."

Her breath was sucked in harshly, and she withdrew even farther across the mattress, so he couldn't feel the silk of her nightgown or the heat of her body.

"That's all you feel for me? You called me precious. I thought that meant you liked me. That you had feelings for me."

"Of course I care about you." His heart lurched at how precarious everything felt all of a sudden. He sensed he was on the verge of a public disgrace when there was only the two of them here in the dark, barely able to read each other's expressions. "I care about you a lot. I *trust* you." To a point, but far more than most people in his life.

She didn't move, but he could feel her gaze trying to penetrate the shadows and read his expression. He felt her confusion and disappointment hitting him in chilly waves.

"I'm not trying to hurt you, Amelia. I'm explaining why I'm careful how deep I let myself fall. This is why someone like Eden seemed a safer bet. I knew I would never feel like this about her."

"Then you shouldn't have tried to marry her!" Her disgust hit him like wet muck. "And thanks for *that* heartfelt compliment. Do you know where *I* come from? A man who reminded me daily that there were other women out there who were better for him, exactly like you're doing right now. Gosh, I'm sooo lucky you picked me, though. Aren't I? Except you *didn't*."

"Amelia." He tried to reach across to her, but she batted his hand away and sat up, throwing off the blankets.

"Do you know what's ironic, Hunter? Gareth kept telling me he loved me and I thought that meant he should want to marry me. When I asked if he would ever propose, he always dodged. You and I *are* married, but you don't love me and you have no plans to do so."

He came up on his elbow. "Do you want me to lie about something like that? The way he did?" Defensiveness shot the question out of him, sending his finger pointing toward the window and the boat on the water while a trail of fiery guilt went down his throat and expanded through his chest.

"No," she acknowledged with a huskiness in her voice. She swallowed, keeping her back to him.

"Once again, you're warning me against having false expectations. That's pretty decent of you. I mean it," she added when he swore under his breath.

She stood.

"Where are you going? I'll sleep somewhere else if you're too angry to share a bed."

"I'm not *angry*," she choked out. "I'm hurt. Crushed. Maybe that's all it is," she said with a pang of weak hope. She sniffed and brushed at her cheek. "Maybe it will wear off in due course and won't hurt so much."

That hit him like a knee in the stomach. He lifted his hand, wanting to grab back something he felt slipping away, but he was too far away. There was only empty air between them. He let his hand fall back onto the blanket, and heaviness coated his heart.

"Lie down. We shouldn't argue about something like this when we're so emotional."

"Oh, are you emotional? How do I tell?" she asked over her shoulder. "You know, it would have been fine if you had simply said you weren't there yet. That you needed more time, but no. You had to tell me that you begrudge the great sex. That it makes you uncomfortable because you think I'm going to use it against you. I don't know what to do with that, Hunter. I only know I can't sleep beside you. Not tonight." She walked out.

He swore again, throat thick with the words he didn't know how to find. He didn't begrudge the sex. He respected it as the force it was. And he cared for her enough that his chest felt hollowed out and achy that he'd hurt her. That she'd chosen to leave their bed and go to Peyton's room.

He glanced at the baby monitor as he heard the soft rustle of her movements in the nursery as she climbed into the bed there. After a moment, he heard a shaken breath. A sniff.

Ah hell. He clenched his eyes shut. That's why she'd left. She wanted to cry. Alone.

CHAPTER THIRTEEN

THE NEXT FEW days were rough. Peyton was cutting her first tooth, crying on and off all day and night. That gave Amelia an excuse for her wan expression and red eyes, as well as a reason to sleep in the nursery.

She wasn't trying to punish Hunter or even avoid him, she just didn't know what to say or how to act around him. She half expected him to accuse her of withholding sex as some sort of power play, but he only asked if she wanted him to cancel his meeting to help with Peyton.

"There's nothing you can do," she said wearily. "She wants me."

Poor Matinder was constantly hovering with teething gel and frozen face cloths at the ready, wringing her hands with helplessness.

"I'll be home by five," he promised, and was.

When he walked into their bedroom and found her pacing before the windows, trying to soothe Peyton, he said, "Still fussing? I'll cancel dinner."

Amelia stared at him, mind blank. It was a broadcast thing, she recollected. A pretty big deal, actually. He was supposed to present awards.

"Did you mention that this morning? I completely forgot." She looked at the clock, noting that she should have started getting ready an hour ago. "You can go without me."

"You've had her all day. I'll take her so you can have a break."

"She doesn't want anyone else to hold her," Amelia said with exasperation.

"You need a break," he said firmly. "Go run a bath." He gently stole Peyton, who began to sob with fresh misery, but she flopped her head onto his shoulder in a bid for comfort.

Amelia didn't want to be alone with her thoughts. She would dwell on things like this, how her husband could make her feel so scorned, yet show her such consideration. It was maddening, but she couldn't help loving him more for it.

As it turned out, she was so shortchanged on sleep, she fell asleep in the tub, waking with a start to tepid water and a still-full glass of wine.

For the first time in days, she spent more than five seconds on her appearance, pulling both thoughts and emotions back together as she dried her hair and touched up her eyebrows and worked moisturizer into her hands and feet.

Was she putting off a difficult conversation? Yes. She and Hunter were due to fly back to Vancouver tomorrow, and she didn't know if she should go with him or if they ought to take a break.

She dressed in wine-colored pedal pushers and a sleeveless mock turtleneck, then went looking for them.

He was in the den off the main lounge that he used as his home office when they were here in the penthouse. Peyton was asleep in his arms, and he was talking on his phone.

"Try that and call me if—"

Some inner radar had him glancing at the door, almost as if he had been watching for her, concerned he might be overheard. Wary stillness came over him.

"I'm in Toronto," he continued evenly, holding her gaze. "We'll stay here until I hear from you. Call me anytime on this number." He ended the call. "Feel better?"

That had sounded exactly like any of his business calls, but something had her skin prickling. "Was that Remy?"

"No." The question seemed to surprise him. "He's in France as far as I know."

"Mmm." She searched his expression, which seemed deliberately stoic. "I thought you had meetings in Vancouver this week?"

"Right. Thank you for the reminder." Was he deliberately avoiding her eyes by glancing at his phone screen? "I have to make some calls to push those back. I'll put Peyton down, then do that. The table is set on the terrace. Start without me." He brushed past her.

She had worked up her courage to address the elephant that had been trampling all over their separate bedrooms for the last few days, and he disappeared before she could even acknowledge it.

Frustrated, she sat down to eat, but he didn't join her. When he finally did, he seemed distracted. Then Peyton woke and Amelia's chance to have an adult conversation with him was gone.

For the first time since their argument, Amelia went to bed in their bedroom as a sort of peace offering, but he wasn't there, and she couldn't get comfortable. Her mind spun for two hours with all the things they weren't saying.

She could have gotten up to find him, she supposed, but she suspected he was sleeping in another room and that was such a painful death knell on their marriage, she didn't want to face it.

He wasn't there when she rose at three to feed Peyton and she flopped straight back to sleep after, still playing catch-up from her recent sleepless nights.

She was bordering on a coma when he gently squeezed her shoulder. "Amelia."

For a moment she was disoriented and only felt the warm joy that always filled her when she opened her eyes to him.

Then she took in the daylight and the fact that he looked like ten miles of dirt road, eyes sunken and face lined.

"Have you been up all night? Is Peyton okay?" She hiked herself onto an elbow.

"She's fine. I changed her and gave her a bottle. Matinder has her."

"Okay. Um…" Her heart lurched. They were really close. His hand was still on her shoulder. It was all she could do not to press her cheek to his hand. Her throat began to burn with apprehension at what might come of this, but… "Should we ta—?"

"I got a call," he said over her. His hand tightened on her shoulder as though he braced her for something. "Jasper is alive. He's on his way here."

If she hadn't been lying on the bed, she would have dropped like a stone. Everything fell away. Wind seemed to rush around as she plummeted through blurred, empty space.

A cold ghost sat in her throat, turning her voice to crushed ice. "Pinch me."

"It's real." He rubbed her shoulder with enough friction to assure her that she was awake.

She was still afraid to believe, but her body reacted, sweeping back the covers. She slapped her feet onto the hardwood floor and stood so fast, her head swam.

"Easy." He steadied her. "He only left Santiago a few hours ago. He won't get here until late tonight. Okay, I know, I know."

She only realized she was shaking and growing limp, breathing so fast her vision was fading, when his arms went around her, catching her before she crumpled to the floor. The tears came so hard and thick, they made her cheeks ache, but there was no stopping them.

"I know, I know," he kept saying, rubbing her back and smoothing her hair.

He didn't know. He couldn't. But when he eased onto the bed and drew her into his lap, cradling her, she clung to him, weeping out all the loss she'd carried this last year.

When she was weak and wrecked, head too heavy to lift, she only had one thought. "I have to phone Dad." Her voice was a rusty nail on a chalkboard.

"I've sent a car for him. I didn't tell him why. Listen." His arms tightened around her. "I didn't know for sure that Jasper was alive until he was in the air. That was his instruction. They had to sneak him out because somewhere in the REM-ex chain of command there are people who don't want him alive. He thought it better to let them think he was dead. Otherwise, they might have come after you and your dad."

She tilted her face up, searching his grim expression, trying to take that in.

"He said he would tell you as much as he can when he gets here, but we have to keep his return secret."

"Anything," she vowed.

He nodded. "Good. Get dressed. I'll dismiss the staff for the day."

She moved through the rest of the day as though walking through gelatin.

A few times she caught Hunter looking at her. They had so much to talk about, but her mind was consumed by Jasper, by willing his flight to arrive safely. Maybe she was even embracing this momentous occasion to avoid thinking about what would happen next with her husband.

Peyton finally, *finally* cut her two bottom teeth. Her swollen gums settled and two sharp white lines appeared. She smiled again, but Amelia still held her for her own comfort, pacing restlessly, arms aching, mind nothing but cotton balls.

Her father turned up, and they had a long hug and a good cry, then it was more waiting. Each minute was a ratchet on a torture device until Amelia was utterly, emotionally exhausted.

Finally, when she was yawning because it was growing late, the elevator dinged.

She stood and held her breath.

A man she barely recognized stepped off the elevator. He wore a bushy beard and was thinner than he'd been even in his high school beanpole days. He had a scar cut into his eyebrow, and his clothes were hanging off his wiry frame, but it was him. It was Jasper. Her brother.

She handed Peyton to Hunter and followed her father across the floor into a big hug that nearly broke her in half. Both of the men closed her in so strongly she couldn't breathe, but she was completely okay with that.

Her father was saying, "Son. My son," and Jasper was whispering a jagged, "I'm sorry. I'm so sorry."

Tobias broke away first, trying to regain his composure by wiping his handkerchief across his cheeks.

Amelia wasn't ready to let go and wrapped both her arms around her brother. He smelled like he had showered in chlorinated water, maybe on the airplane? She didn't care. The chemical smell imprinted on her as the best fragrance in the world, one that swelled her heart with joy.

"I can't believe you're really here."

Jasper nearly lifted her off the ground as he squeezed her. "All thanks to that flop of a cake I made for you when you hit puberty."

"What?" She lifted her wet face, vaguely remembering telling Hunter about that.

"A stranger turned up claiming to work for your husband, but I didn't even know you were married. It felt like a setup, so I told him he had the wrong guy. Then he told me about the cake. I knew you wouldn't have shared that with anyone you didn't trust completely."

She looked to Hunter, starting to realize exactly what he had done for her. He stood there all gorgeous and tailored, even though his expression was pulled into an emotive grimace while he watched their reunion. He cradled their daughter, always the tender, attentive father he had told her he wanted to be. In fact, his dedication to her and her family was so deep, he had found her brother and reunited her with him.

She'd been so hurt after their fight, and now it seemed like a huge waste of her energy to be angry. If this was Hunter's version of caring, his unfettered love might be too strong to withstand. She was having trouble bearing the emotions swamping her as it was.

Just then, Tobias blew his nose with the goose honk that had been a mainstay of her childhood. It was such a familiar sound of home, it didn't even alarm Peyton and busted Amelia and Jasper into laughing so hard, they doubled over, breathless and crying. It was too strong a reaction for such a silly thing, but it broke the tension and allowed her to draw Jasper the rest of the way into the apartment.

"You must be Hunter," Jasper said, offering his hand.

"Good to meet you. And this is your niece. Peyton."

Peyton was a sturdy little bundle these days, keeping her head up and her attention alert. She fixed her eyes on Jasper, fist in her mouth.

As if she recognized one of her own, she pointed her wet hand at Jasper and smiled, showing off the glint of white on her gums.

"Hey," he said shakily. "We have the same name." As he took her, Jasper glanced at Amelia with a gentle scold for being so sentimental as to give her daughter his middle name and for bringing fresh tears to his eyes.

"I was going to come to Chile and look for you myself, but I found out I was carrying her—"

"I was doing my best to stay lost. You wouldn't have— *Ouch.* That's quite a grip, kid." He pried her fist loose from his beard and shifted her against his shoulder, letting her curl her hand around his finger instead.

"Why did you have to hide?" Tobias demanded, easing into a chair.

"Sit," Hunter invited with a wave.

"Thanks. I'm exhausted."

Jasper sank onto the sofa, and Amelia perched right beside him.

"I am *so* sorry I let you believe I was dead." Jasper included both her and Tobias in his remorseful look. "I can't explain it all. Not yet. I can't even stay. The man Hunter sent—I won't give you his name. Hunter has arranged for him to take me to an undisclosed location. Thanks for the lawyer, by the way," Jasper said to Hunter. "I'll swear some statements into evidence before I go public that I'm alive. It's easier to leave a man for dead in remote mountains a continent away than it will be once there are charges pending. It'll be dangerous for me at first, and ugly for all of you for a while. That's why I want you at arm's length. Hunter knows how to reach me if something happens, but until I go public, I'm still dead. Got it?"

"I guess." Amelia's lips wouldn't stay steady enough to speak. "I really missed you, though. I don't want you to go away again."

"I won't go far. I missed you, too." He looped his free arm across her shoulders and hugged her into his side. Then he let her take Peyton. "But it has to be this way."

"Okay," Amelia hiccuped, recognizing his stubborn look. Arguing would be futile.

"Dad?" Jasper asked, moving toward Tobias.

"You're alive, son. That's all that matters to me." Tobias stood and hugged him. "Come home as soon as you can."

"I will." With a final pet of Peyton's hair and a kiss on Amelia's cheek, Jasper left.

"Was that even real? It feels like a dream." Amelia sank back onto the sofa, still holding Peyton, face pale, but with a light behind her eyes that Hunter hadn't seen since he'd met her.

He squeezed her shoulder.

"Can I get you a drink, Tobias?" he asked as the older man slumped back into an armchair as though he'd run a marathon today.

Tobias rubbed his face.

"I'm trying to decide if I'm sleeping here or catching a lift home so I can sleep in my own bed."

"I'll take you in the morning," Amelia said. "Peyton and I will come stay for, um…" She glanced uncertainly at Hunter, then down at their daughter.

Hunter's heart swerved in his chest. The morning after she had told him she loved him, he'd gotten the first inkling that Jasper might have been found. Hunter had wanted to tell her, but after disappointing her so badly that night, he couldn't bring himself to raise her hopes if they were about to be dashed again.

With Peyton so fussy, Amelia had had her hands full without his toying further with her emotions. He had focused on relaying what information he could to convince Jasper to trust his emissary and come home.

Hunter was glad, so glad that he'd been able to find Jasper, but he was aware that Jasper's brief visit didn't undo the hurt he'd caused Amelia.

"You'll be heading back to Vancouver, won't you?" Tobias was saying.

"That was the plan," Hunter said carefully.

"It bothers me you're alone at home," Amelia said in a subdued voice.

"We have plenty of room if you want to come to Vancouver with us," Hunter said, not for the first time. Or the last. "There's a room ready for you."

"I'm not alone in Goderich. I have my coffee with the boys every morning," Tobias reminded her, then grew sheepish. "And I've taken to having pie with Mo's sister, Ola, on Sunday afternoons. Sometimes we have the early bird special at Thursday's on Thursday. Don't get any ideas." He shook a warning finger. "She's a widow with kids who have grown and left the nest, same as me. We keep each other company, is all. It's someone new to talk to who hasn't heard all our same old yarns, but I wouldn't want her feeling lonely if I weren't there." He wore a self-conscious blush on his cheeks.

"Oh. That's nice. I'm happy if you're happy, Dad." Amelia blinked in bemusement.

"And we'd be happy for you to bring her for a visit if that works sometime, too," Hunter said. "I can make arrangements anytime. Just let me know."

"I will, thanks. I've decided to hit the hay," Tobias said, standing and heaving a sigh. "It's been a long day, and it's catching up to me."

Amelia rose, and they said their good-nights. Then she disappeared to put Peyton down for the night.

Hunter poured himself a drink, bracing himself for the reckoning that couldn't be avoided. *Peyton and I will come stay...*

She didn't want to come to Vancouver with him.

His guts roiled with the dark irony of her rejection. His greatest fear had been that Amelia would hold some sort of power over him, and she did. Knowing she was angry with him, and worse, knowing he deserved it, had been eating into him like acid.

He was every bit as enamored with and susceptible to her as his father had been Irina.

The difference was, Amelia was sensitive and supportive and *loving*. How had he seen that as a threat? Her heart was the most precious thing she could offer him, and he'd been a blind fool to throw it back at her the way he had.

No wonder she wanted to leave him.

Now he'd ruined it. He'd seen how completely she loathed the last man who hadn't given her the respect her love deserved.

Her footsteps on the stairs had him turning to pour her wine and top up his scotch.

"Oh my God. Thank you," she sighed as he handed her the glass. She took a sip. "And *thank you*." Her eyes glossed with emotion. "I don't know how to even process that you brought my brother back from the dead."

"I threw money at a problem and hoped for the best. Fortunately, that's what we got."

"I'm still very grateful," she said sincerely.

Grateful enough to stay? The pain down his breastbone was sharp as a fracture.

"I can't imagine what it cost you," she was saying, as if he cared about the money. "Finding him. The chartered flight... And his legal bills?" Her brow twisted with anxiety. "That's not your responsibility, Hunter. Dad has said many times that he can remortgage the house—"

"Don't even think it. There will be a settlement. It will be huge. Trust me. Anything I give Jasper will be a loan." It stung that she didn't want his money. How was this still a bone of contention between them? "You would help my sister in any way you could. I know that."

"I would," she agreed absently, then winced. "But it sounds like our family will drag yours into the spotlight *again*. That's why I thought going to live with Dad would be a good idea. Wouldn't it be better for you if we said we were on a trial separation—"

"Better?" he choked. "How would it be better for me if my wife and daughter leave me?"

"I..." Her shoulders slumped. "I know you want Peyton close to you, but—"

"I want you!" he shouted, then clacked his teeth together. He glanced toward the stairs as he recalled that her father was trying to sleep. Pressure filled his head and his throat and his chest. Urgency. *Fear.*

"Dad wears earplugs so Peyton doesn't wake

him." Amelia hugged herself as she eyed him warily. "I know that we click, chemistry-wise. I just don't know how that can be enough when you're going to all this trouble on my behalf."

"Enough?" He ran a hand down his face, wondering how she could make him feel so callow and misunderstood. "I didn't search for him so I could get laid, Amelia. It was the right thing to do and it might not have worked out as well as it did, but I wanted answers for you, one way or another."

"Because you care about me." She sat down, hand shaking as she abandoned her wine on the coffee table. "I know you do and I've been churlish, acting as though you don't give me everything I need when you *do*. I realize that. Words are cheap. Actions are real and the way you act is…loving. It's okay if you don't say the words or feel it the way I do."

"Don't be so damned forgiving!" he burst out, hating himself in that moment. "Do you know how I would have reacted if I told you I loved you and you said, *That's nice*? I would throw up my heart and wonder what reason there was for continuing with my sorry life. I would call you a coward when I can see with my own eyes that you love me." He pointed at his eyes. They were stinging with gathering tears. His throat was on fire, barely able to mutter, "Even if you were too stubborn and scared to say the words."

She tucked her chin and bit her trembling lips into a line, blinking wet lashes.

"Actions *are* real," he noted. "The things you do for me… I don't need a business partner for a wife. I need *you*. By my side. *Taking* my side. You keep me grounded and give me someone to come home to. You make every one of my houses feel like a home. If you're not here, then I guess I'm moving to Goderich, because my home is wherever you are. I need you in my life. I need you to keep me from being a distrustful jerk and to help me see the good in this world. You *are* the good in this world. You're the good in *my* world."

The tears brimming her lashes began to trickle down her cheeks, but she managed to sniff, "And Peyton."

"She wouldn't be here without you, would she?"

She released a shaky chuckle. "I'm starting to think you really do love me."

"I'm starting to think so, too," he said humbly. Contritely. "I think I love you more than either of us realize."

He waited for the cavernous vulnerability to hit him, but saying those words didn't make him feel defenseless. They filled him with something strong and certain and right. Like lifeblood. Like air. Necessary and energizing.

He had been so afraid of what she would take from him if he let himself fall for her. Instead, he wanted to give her everything. Not in a foolish way. Not as an infantile means of keeping her, but because he wanted her to know what she meant to him. Because he wanted her to thrive so she could be with him always.

He walked across and knelt before her, cupping her cheeks.

"I love you," he said, feeling the words vibrate from the depths of his chest, radiating outward to his fingertips and toes. The only way it broke anything inside him was to crack the wall around his heart. Rather than feeling unguarded, he felt *free*.

"I love you, too." Her mouth trembled. "So much."

He stood and drew her up with him, closing his arms around her, needing as much of her touching him as possible. He needed the taste of her unsteady lips against his. The dampness of her tears against his cheek and the press of her heartbeat to his chest.

Her thumb swept across his clenched eye. There was dampness there, and he only held her closer, unashamed by how much of his love was seeping out of him to land on her.

"I thought I would lose you," he confessed. "I didn't know how I would bear it."

"I'm here. I will be. Always."

"Same. Always."

They kept making promises between kisses, slowly making their way up the stairs to their room. To their bed.

And when they made love, it was pure love, each caress and kiss a vow. It was a celebration of their bodies and their soul-deep connection.

When the shimmering clench of climax began to grip them, she traced his ear and said with a pang of doubt, "You're still waiting for me."

"Because I'm a gentleman, love."

Which made her laugh. She twisted and he was lost to the throes of climax, groaning and thrusting, dragging her with him into the delirious storm.

EPILOGUE

Two days later

HUNTER ARRIVED IN Goderich as they were sitting down to dinner. Amelia hurried to rise and meet him at the door even though they'd only been apart the one night. She had wanted a little more time with her father after the upheaval of Jasper's return, so she had driven home with him yesterday.

She had also been anxious to vet her father's sweetheart. Mo's sister, Ola, was an absolute doll. Amelia would worry about him a lot less when she returned to Vancouver, knowing the pair were keeping each other company.

"Hey." Hunter greeted her with an intimate smile and a warm tone and a lingering kiss that curled her toes against the welcome mat. "Traffic getting out of the city was a nightmare or I would have made better time."

"It's okay. Supper's almost on the table, so this is perfect."

"You must be Ola," he said as he greeted the

woman with gray hair and a tender touch as she cradled Peyton. "Tobias." He nodded at her father, then touched his daughter's hair. "Hello, bean sprout. I missed you."

Peyton picked up her head, but her eyes were still heavy from her recent nap.

It was a pleasant meal with plenty of chatter as Amelia and Ola continued getting to know each other, but Amelia noticed Hunter wasn't saying much.

After he drove Ola home and her father had gone to bed, she put Peyton down for the night and joined Hunter on the couch.

"Are you okay? You've been quiet."

"Plotting my revenge against your father if he decides to marry Ola," he claimed wryly, staring into the drink he had yet to finish.

"Just desserts," she said lightly, taking heart from the fact that he was making jokes.

She brought her knees up under her and leaned into him, wrapping her arm across his shoulders as she kissed the side of his face.

"How did it go with Remy?" she asked gently.

"Fine." He chased it with a swallow of whiskey.

Okay. She wouldn't press. Today had been the only window of time for the men to connect. Hunter had been planning to come with her yesterday, but heard at the last minute that Remy and Eden had come into Toronto. He had sent Amelia ahead and lingered to catch up with his friend.

She started to withdraw her arm from around him.

"Don't do that." He set aside his drink and swiveled her into his lap. "I'm being cryptic because he told me some things he never shared before. I don't want to break his confidence."

"I don't expect you to." She nestled her shoulder beneath his arm, relaxing as she understood his walls were protecting his friend, not himself.

"Also, he gave me Eden's engagement ring. What am I supposed to do with that?" He shook his head in baffled annoyance. "It's in the safe at the penthouse. I'll unload it as soon as I can."

"It doesn't bother me. I'm just glad you're on speaking terms again."

"We weren't *not* on speaking terms. He had a lot going on and wasn't ready to talk until now. I respect that," Hunter summed up pensively.

"Are he and Eden happy?" She discovered that she hoped they were.

"Not happy the way we're happy." Hunter dragged her bottom more fully into his lap and dropped his smug smile onto her lips, turning it into a tender kiss. "But who could be?"

"I know, right?" She played with the buttons on his shirt, thinking about releasing them.

"The whole drive here, I was thinking how lucky I am." His hand traced absent circles on her back. "Lucky Remy dragged me away that weekend last year. Lucky you joined us. I'm damned lucky your father interrupted my wedding to the wrong woman. I don't want revenge against him," he assured her with a grave look. "I want to give him a kidney if he needs it. I owe him a lot."

"We gave him a grandchild. That's a pretty close second." She was grinning with amusement, but growing misty with emotive tears. "I'd suggest we give him another, but honestly, I need this one weaned and sleeping through the night before we have that conversation."

"I want that, too. The second baby and the uninterrupted sleep." He grew more contemplative, tucking her head beneath his chin as he absently sifted his fingers through the curtain of her hair before warming the back of her neck with his palm. "I want to go through the pregnancy with you and be there when you're swearing at me through labor. I want time with *you* before we bring another personality into the mix. I do love you, you know. So much, I can hardly breathe sometimes."

"I do know." Her eyes were wet and stinging, her smile wide and unsteady. She felt his love with everything in her and could hardly breathe herself. "But I don't get tired of hearing it. Or feeling it." She pressed closer suggestively.

"Allow me to demonstrate, then."

"Please do."

He lifted her into his arms and carried her to the bedroom, where he did exactly that.

* * * * *

Swept away by Cinderella's Secret Baby?
*Then make sure to look out for the next instalment
in the Four Weddings and a Baby quartet,
coming soon.*

*In the meantime, explore these other
Dani Collins stories!*

Her Impossible Baby Bombshell
Married for One Reason Only
Manhattan's Most Scandalous Reunion
One Snowbound New Year's Night
Cinderella for the Miami Playboy
Innocent in Her Enemy's Bed

Available now!

#4049 HER CHRISTMAS BABY CONFESSION
Secrets of the Monterosso Throne
by Sharon Kendrick

Accepting a flight home from a royal wedding with Greek playboy Xanthos is totally out of character for Bianca. Yet when they're suddenly snowbound together, Bianca chooses to embrace their deliciously dangerous chemistry, just once...only to find herself carrying a shocking secret!

#4050 A WEEK WITH THE FORBIDDEN GREEK
by Cathy Williams

Grace Brown doesn't have time to fantasize about her boss, Nico Doukas...never mind how attractive he is! But when she accompanies him on a business trip, the earth-shattering desire between them makes keeping things professional impossible...

#4051 THE PRINCE'S PREGNANT SECRETARY
The Van Ambrose Royals
by Emmy Grayson

Clara is shocked to discover she's carrying her royal boss's baby! The last thing she wants is to become Prince Alaric's convenient princess, but marriage will protect their child from scandal. Can their honeymoon remind them that more than duty binds them?

#4052 RECLAIMING HIS RUNAWAY CINDERELLA
by Annie West

After years of searching for the heiress who fled just hours after their convenient marriage, Cesare finally tracks Ida down. Intent on finalizing their divorce, he hadn't counted on the undeniable attraction between them! Dare they indulge in the wedding night they never had?

#4053 NINE MONTHS AFTER THAT NIGHT
Weddings Worth Billions
by Melanie Milburne
Billionaire hotelier Jack is blindsided when he discovers the woman he spent one mind-blowing night with is in the hospital... having his baby! Marriage is the only way to make sure his daughter has the perfect upbringing. But only *if* Harper accepts his proposal...

#4054 UNWRAPPING HIS NEW YORK INNOCENT
Billion-Dollar Christmas Confessions
by Heidi Rice
Alex Costa doesn't trust *anyone*. Yet he cannot deny the attraction when he meets sweet, innocent Ellie. Keeping her at arm's length could prove impossible when the fling they embark on unwraps the most intimate of secrets...

#4055 SNOWBOUND IN HER BOSS'S BED
by Marcella Bell
When Miriam is summoned to Benjamin Silver's luxurious Aspen chalet, she certainly doesn't expect a blizzard to leave her stranded there for Hanukkah! Until the storm passes, she must battle her scandalous and ever-intensifying attraction to her boss...

#4056 THEIR DUBAI MARRIAGE MAKEOVER
by Louise Fuller
Omar refuses to allow Delphi to walk away from him. His relentless drive has pushed her away and now he must convince her to return to Dubai to save their marriage. But is he ready to reimagine everything he believed their life together would be?

YOU CAN FIND MORE INFORMATION ON UPCOMING HARLEQUIN TITLES, FREE EXCERPTS AND MORE AT HARLEQUIN.COM.

HPCNMRB0922

*Cesare intends to finalize his divorce to his runaway
bride, Ida. Yet he hadn't counted on discovering Ida's
total innocence in their marriage sham. Or on the
attraction that rises swift and hot between them...
Dare they indulge in the wedding night they never had?*

*Read on for a sneak preview of
Annie West's 50th book for Harlequin Presents,*
Reclaiming His Runaway Cinderella

"Okay. We're alone. Why did you come looking for me?"

"I thought that was obvious."

How could Ida have forgotten the intensity of that
brooding stare? Cesare's eyes bored into hers as if seeking
out misdemeanors or weaknesses.

But she'd done him no wrong. She didn't owe him
anything and refused to be cowed by that flinty gaze. Ida
shoved her hands deep in her raincoat pockets and raised
her eyebrows.

"It's been a long day, Cesare. I'm not in the mood for
guessing games. Just tell me. What do you want?"

He crossed the space between them in a couple of deceptively easy strides. Deceptive because his expression told her it was the prowl of a predator.

"To sort out our divorce, of course."

"We're still married?"

Don't miss
Reclaiming His Runaway Cinderella
available November 2022 wherever
Harlequin Presents books and ebooks are sold.

Harlequin.com

HARLEQUIN

Heartfelt or thrilling, passionate or uplifting—Harlequin is more than just happily-ever-after.

With twelve different series to choose from and new books available every month, you are sure to find stories that will move you, uplift you, inspire and delight you.

HNEWS2021